Richard Crawley

Horse & Foot

Pilgrims to Parnassus

Richard Crawley

Horse & Foot
Pilgrims to Parnassus

ISBN/EAN: 9783337287801

Printed in Europe, USA, Canada, Australia, Japan

Cover: Foto ©Andreas Hilbeck / pixelio.de

More available books at **www.hansebooks.com**

HORSE & FOOT.

PILGRIMS TO PARNASSUS.

BY RICHARD CRAWLEY.

" I'll not march through Coventry with them, that's flat."

LONDON :

JOHN CAMDEN HOTTEN, PICCADILLY.

1868.

PREFACE.

BY way of preface to this Satire, I need only remark that I have no acquaintance with the persons mentioned in it, or indeed with any one in the literary world : I have written independently.

DEDICATION.

TO F. W. B.

THE morning's child, the painted butterfly,
    Lives scarce one day, but lives it in the sun ;
More days are ours, yet, by the time we die,
How much more sunshine have we looked upon !
Sighing in Youth, because To-morrow lingers ;
In Age, because fair Yesterday has fled,
We let the present good escape our fingers,
And wildly grasp at future joys instead.
But, oh ! what's gone is surely past regretting,
And, if you'll trust philosophers and sages,
What's coming 's usually not worth the getting,
So let us take the pleasures of our ages ;
    For C— a system, M— a face that's new,
    Me summer days and winter nights with you.

HORSE & FOOT;

OR,

PILGRIMS TO PARNASSUS.

WHEN loud for beer each honest pauper storms,
    When men like robins stand agape for worms ;
When bards in legions throng the Muse's hill,
And verse, like sewage, chokes the sacred rill ;
5 Curst be the man, who in these wretched times
Gives many children to the state, or rhymes.

OF these two criminals the last is worst
Yet mercy, Mill[1] and Phœbus, 'tis my first !

---

[1] See Mr. J. S. Mill's " Political Economy," vol. i., p. 458 :—
" Little improvement can be expected in morality until the pro-

I've license now ; if others I beget,

10   No doubt a jail or two 'll be standing yet.

For Mill, a prophet and a man of parts,

Adapts his doctrine to our hardened hearts ;

Gives mortals two, and parsons three or four,

Though five's sheer folly, and ' brute instinct ' more :

15   And I'll uphold when men and gods have done,

That e'en a poet has his right to one.

Yet haste, good people, ere the sentence fall,

Soon 'twill be crime to propagate at all :

---

ducing of large families is regarded with the same feelings as drunkenness or any other physical excess.   But while the aristo-cracy and clergy are foremost to set the example of this kind of incontinence, what can be expected of the poor ?"

Again, p. 438, this conduct is described as :—" A degrading slavery to a brute instinct in one of the persons concerned, and most commonly in the other helpless submission to a revolting abuse of power."

A heroic attempt to upset the tyranny, which Mr. Mill so justly stigmatises, and its failure, is commemorated by Prior in his tale of " Paulo Purgante."

Soon Mill's successor in his glorious course
20 Will make the nation bachelor by force.

WHILE here Statistics, and here Nature calls,
While Prudence checks me, and while Fame enthrals :
Ere Phœbus hides indignant in the deep,
Ere Patmore[2] drones the last, last muse to sleep ;
25 Ere, vanquished in the fratricidal strife,
The last goose yields its feathers, and its life ;
Ere cautious crows the coming doom foresee,
And jackdaws fly from Woolner[3] and from me :
Ere paper rise my modest means above,
30 While ink still sells for copper or for love ;
'Tis fixed, I loose my shallop from the shore,
And give to Folly's court one fool the more.

[2] Mr. Coventry Patmore the author of " The Angel in the House," and other verses.

[3] Mr. Thomas Woolner, the author of a poem called " My Beautiful Lady."

WHEN heedless Jove in sport or spite began,
And out of clay[4] and nectar moulded man,
35 The mighty creature, if old tales be true,
First fed on acorns as the monkeys do;
And so for ages dwelt beside the springs,
Remote from bakers, booksellers, and kings.
At last he learned the genial fields to sow,
40 And harnessed wife or oxen to the plough,
Brewed beer, got drunk, and tasted Sirloin's might,
Waxed fat, trapped geese, and straight began to write.

SINCE then like raging fire the mischief spread,
Odes in each eye, and nonsense in each head,
45 Till scribbling got engrafted in the wood,
And grew a vice inveterate to the blood.

---

[4] That is to say that man was made after dinner. Out of the wetter clods were formed Germans; out of the dust, Frenchmen; while from the firmest and finest pieces, arose Englishmen. After supper, when a more generous fluid had been brought in, an odd-looking lump was found by Mars in Venus' lap, which Mercury handed to Jove. With it he made Irishmen.

Go then, young templar, or more sprightly cit,
The world thine oyster, and thy knife thy wit;
Whoe'er thou art uneasy with thy state,
50 Who wouldst at once be opulent and great;
Go, search broad nature, fly from zone to zone,
And find the prodigy to print unknown,
Then cage the monster, call the world to stare,
And shine the happiest showman of the fair.

55 BUT no, 'tis vain for such a thing to look,
For, soon or late, each biped writes a book;
" Leaves from my Journal," " What I did not see
In Norway, France, Peru, or Italy;"
Some stagnant pamphlet on the coming storm,
60 Stray thoughts, and leaden Essays on Reform;
Some sonnets printed at a friend's request,
That friend a lunatic or rogue at best;
Who daily writhing on the listener's wheel,
Vowed that the world what he had felt should feel,
65 And madly soothed his misanthropic mind,
By knowing torture common to the kind.

Yet though man's nothing but a joke at best,
'Tis true there's something serious in the jest;
So in this journey through the realms of rhyme,

70　I'll take it all in earnest for the time,
And changing still, as humour sways the lyre,
Be wroth, sad, merry, careless, or admire.

There was a time, ere Trollope[5] learned to spell,

---

[5] Mr. Thomas Anthony Trollope, the chief of those popular
novelists, " who," I am quoting from Mr. Mill, " teach nothing
but (what is already too soon learnt from actual life) lessons of
worldliness, with, at most, the huckstering virtues which con-
duce to getting on in the world; and, for the first time, perhaps, in history, the youth of both sexes of the educated classes
are universally growing up unromantic. What will come in
mature age from such a youth, the world has not yet had time
to see."

Again, from the same essay :—"The time was, when it was
thought that the best and most appropriate office of fictitious
narrative was to awaken high aspirations, by the representation
in interesting circumstances, of characters conformable indeed
to human nature, but whose actions and sentiments were of a
more generous and loftier cast than are ordinarily to be met
with by everybody in every-day life. But now-a-days nature

When S. G. O.[6] wrote seldom or wrote well,

75   When Swinburne[7] only lusted after tarts,

When Beales[8] was yet a Bachelor of Arts:

Ere Broad Church rose to make logicians stare,

That medley of St. Paul and St. Voltaire ;

---

and probability are thought to be violated, if there be shown to the reader, in the personages with whom he is called upon to sympathise, characters on a larger scale than himself, or than the persons he is accustomed to meet at a dinner and a quadrille party."

I ought to remark that it is I, not Mr. Mill, who apply these observations to Mr. Trollope.

[6] S. G. O., the irrepressible correspondent of the "Times." For the sake of his parishioners I hope his doctrine is more orthodox than his grammar, and his sermons shorter than his letters.

[7] Mr. Algernon Charles Swinburne, author of "Atalanta in Calydon," "Chastelard," "Poems and Ballads," &c.

[8] Mr. Edmond Beales, Master of Arts and Oratory. But it is superfluous to describe him. As was said, gentle reader, of his great predecessor, if he will pardon me the comparison, " not to know him argues thyself unknown."

When Alma Mater still young Genius fed,

80　　Nor suckled slaves[9] and editors[10] instead ;

---

[9] I here allude to the debasing system of competitive examination, which, as far as its influence extends, is fast extinguishing all freedom of study and true love of the arts in the Universities and elsewhere.

[10] Our fathers read the classics as a Literature, their sons regard them as a storehouse of Grammar. This may be progress ; it is certainly not improvement. Lord Chesterfield said that a Frenchman, with the manners of his nation, and possessed of a proper fund of genius and virtue, would be the greatest of God's works. So, methinks, I can hear some pedant exclaim that a Grammarian, with the knowledge of his class, and a proper leaven of taste and enthusiasm, would be the first of scholars. To Lord Chesterfield, it was objected, that his Lordship seemed to regard the fund of genius and virtue somewhat in the light of an extra ; and to the other, I would remark that he appears to look upon taste and enthusiasm as at best harmless luxuries.

Of course critical scholarship has its place, but it is essentially a subordinate one : for my own part I read my Æschylus with just as much pleasure, before I could pass an examination in his plays as afterwards ; and if I were Horace, I should beguile the tedium of Elysium, by tormenting the souls of my commentators.

Ere Quaker[11] Wordsworth fettered English song,

Though oft his practice proved his preaching wrong :

When poets poetry in nature sought,

When nature was, and pedantry was not ;

---

[11] Part of Wordsworth's poetry no one can admire more than myself; but I cannot help thinking that his critical opinions have exercised a most degrading influence over our literature. He is seldom mean or vulgar himself, but his poetical descendants are both, and it was he who taught them to be so. He has been called the poet of nature, but without much justice; his view of her was exceedingly narrow ; and while professing to free poetry from the artificial trammels imposed upon it by Pope, he tried to confine it to the mountains of Westmoreland, and the petty though simple existences of the boors that inhabit them. There is little melody or life in his compositions ; he is often undoubtedly dull, and to me there has always been something effeminate and unmanly both in the man and his works. As far as I have been able to observe, he is most popular with the critics : the public read him rather as a duty than a pleasure, and though he occasionally extorts their admiration, he is scarcely ever a favourite. Those who like him best, are usually by nature more addicted to prose than poetry ; the sort of people who are not too strict to go out, but who think dramatic readings both safer and more improving than the theatre.

85 When every reader knew the rules of art,
    For nought was needed but a feeling heart,
    And hearts still blossomed in our English ground,
    And life and motion in our veins were found.
    But now, alas, a heavy change has come !
90 Far wanders Genius from his ancient home,
    And mute, or exiled on a foreign shore
    Still wafts his madness, and his music o'er,
    Her singer still, her citizen no more.

    SHADES of the great, on whose enchanting tongue
95 The men of Spain and of Trafalgar hung !
    Who once these cities and these fields among,
    Towered vast and free the demigods of song ;
    Our kindred still, but heirs of other powers,
    And other stature than these mates of ours ;
100 Confessed a mortal, and a heavenly birth,
    Your lyres were heaven's, but still they spake of earth ;
    The tale is old, and with our race began,
    And ever young,[12] for ever born with man ;

    _____

    [12] Nothing can be more absurd than the ideas which many

His Hope ye sang, Love, Passion, Hate, and Fear,
105 And all the chances of his strange career ;
And still ye sang, and each one held his breath,
In silence sweet and motionless as death :
Grief for a moment all his pains forgot,
And spared a tear to mourn another's lot ;
110 On Joy awhile, soft Melancholy lay,
A sunny cloud upon an April day :
Grey threescore listened, and grew young again,
And beardless youths lived out the lives of men :
Ye ceased, and Fancy's holiday is o'er,
115 And iron Fact oppresses us once more.

AND ye, ye modern bards, what themes are yours !
Faith, physics, metaphysics, and the sewers ;

---

writers of the present day have of progress. If we confine
our view to machinery and so forth, the advance that mankind
has made seems enormous ; if to man himself, scarcely worth
thinking about : we sleep, eat, and travel very differently from
our ancestors, but in essentials, man is in all nations and ages
the same. Otherwise Homer's poetry would be as obsolete as
Thales' physical speculations.

Bad squires, worse workmen, population's strife,
And all the accidents[13] of plaguestruck life !
120 What's worse, the social or the household evil ?
And who made man, God, nature, or the devil ?
The cursed past, the blessed age that's coming,
The wrongs of tinkers, and the rights of women :
Such dregs as ooze from Congreve's muddy pen,
125 And all that headaches give to mortal men,
Invade the hours to wit and wisdom due,
And damn to dulness Morley's new review.[14]

SHALL themes like these usurp a Marmion's[15] praise,
And bards like you from Byron tear the bays,

---

[13] The word "accident" is here used in its philosophical sense as opposed to "essence."

[14] "The Fortnightly Review," edited by Mr. John Morley.

[15] Scott's poetical faculty was perhaps not of the highest order, but Jeffrey was undoubtedly right, when he called the battle in Marmion "the best of all the poetical battles that have been fought since the days of Homer." It is worth ten years of peaceful life to read it.

130 Nor Satire lurk a lion in your ways?

" Why not ! great Dryden's on the shelf forgot,

And Pope—he's judged—smug Progress knows him not :

We read not Dryden,"

What shall Dryden do ?

" Nor Pope,"

Alas for Dulness and for you !

135 " Peace to the pigmies of a former time,

" Their thoughts were light, and lightly rode in rhyme :

" Our souls are freighted with a heavier stuff,

" Blank be the verse, it can't be blank enough ;

" Buchanan's[16] blank, but let him blanker grow,

140 " And Jean[17] surpass the blankest that we know.

" 'Tis true a jingle pleased our fathers well,

" But then our ears are longer by an ell,

---

[16] Mr. Robert Buchanan, author of "Idylls of Inverburn,"
" London Poems," &c.

[17] Miss Jean Ingelow, authoress of the "Story of Doom,"
and other Poems.

" Our senses sharper, and more trained our powers,

" A truer, subtler melody is ours :

145 " Their ghosts, 'tis whispered, glide our groves about,

" And half our noblest music ne'er find out ;

" Still doubt o'er Arnold, and to measuring fall,

" And over Taylor[18] never doubt at all.

" Yet there are many mansions in the house,

150 " Should your friends care with Woolner to carouse ?

" The hall is open to their humbler hope —"

Nay, hold—'tis better to be damned with Pope.

But hark, let Dickson,[19] all unused to hear,

And Odger prick up a seditious ear,

---

[18] Mr. Henry Taylor, author of " Philip Van Artevelde," and other plays.

[19] Lieutenant-Colonel Dickson, a gentleman whose military title divides with Mr. Beales' University degree the admiration of the Reform League. Perhaps, after all, there is something more truly imposing in the plain simplicity of the name " Odger." Either patriot is more accustomed to talk than to listen.

155 Which modern mildness leaves upon his head,
 And curses nature and its own instead ;
 Good news ! for Browning[20] like a rebel comes,
 With bells rung backward, and with beating drums ;
 No lackey he, no Muses' minister,
160 But glorious Anarchy's adventurer :
 Let other drivellers seek the quire to join,
 And basely reign as regents to the Nine,
 Their title own, and to the laws conform,
 But sturdy Robert tries the hill by storm.
165 A painted Sphinx upon his sleeve he wears,
 A painted Sphinx his rebel banner bears ;
 She from the cradle called him for her own,
 And her he destines for the Muses' throne ;
 Her throne by right, and only theirs by wrong,
170 Got in wild times of conquest for a song.

 FOR this a mercenary troop he hires
 Of words cast out of scientific quires ;

---

[20] Mr. Robert Browning, author of "Sordello," "Para-
celsus," "Christmas Eve," and a number of plays and poems.

Each lewd expression of the baser sort,

Each inky pedant still o'erlooked at Court,

175 Each rugged outlaw from the realms of rhyme,

In awkward squads that never marched in time :

Phrases seduced from business and from prose,

Or kept by botanists to scare the crows ;

Each hunched monster melancholic grown

180 With pining in a Lexicon alone ;

Their ammunition terrible to see,

A paste of Science and Theology,[21]

Much loved by those whom Alma Mater weans,

And centuries escaping from their teens.

185 All these he draws, and drills the horrid line,

And bastinadoes into discipline ;

While for reserve a convict force appears,

Whom even Barham[22] broke for mutineers !

---

[21] The poem called " Christmas Eve," in particular, is full of ideas which in my opinion would be far better conveyed in a fugitive treatise on divinity.

[22] Mr. Thomas Barham, the clever author of the " Ingoldsby Legends." His talent in rhyming is well known.

He bids the bagpipe jangle for the fight,
190 And leads them on beneath the cloud of night.

So let him fare, lost rebel though he be,
The noblest, greatest of the lost ones he ;
He leaves afar the ruck of those who fell,
And towers like Satan 'midst the mob of Hell.

195 So let him fare—while Fancy leaves the track,
And brings me Horace, and my childhood back,
When I, beneath a canopy of birch,
He, in the fond lap of the frump Research,
Together journeyed to Brundisium,
200 I wished we never to that town[23] had come,

---

[23] Thus described by Horace in the fifth satire of his first
book :—

> ——" oppidulum, quod versu dicere non est,
> Signis perfacile est: venit vilissima rerum
> Hic aqua ; sed panis longe pulcherrimus, ultra
> Callidus ut soleat humeris portare viator ;
> Nam Canusi lapidosus."

This, it must be acknowledged, is a very pretty difficulty ;
nor have the commentators been wanting to the occasion.

That tipsy spot, where chalkless bread is sold,

And common water must be bought with gold :

By different names to different Germans known,

And each more dull and crabbed than their own ;

205 Built by dead ushers for the schoolboy's curse,

And deaf to Horace, melody, and verse.

But wiser now, tho' sadder than before,

I blame the poet, but the place no more :

More Browning knows than Horace ever knew,

210 He first has shown what Poetry can do.

Had Browning[24] travelled to that town forlorn,

Some fewer scars a tender part had borne ;

They first quote all the instances in which other poets, Latin
or Greek, have recoiled before a proper name, or complained
of the dearness of water; and then fall to guessing the name
of the village ; Orelli fights for Equotutium, Walcknaer with
Wesseling to back him for some other, and so forth.

[24] Mr. Browning is subject to a sort of St. Vitus' dance of
rhymes, which constantly distorts the features of his poetry just
at the wrong moment. But he would have matched Equotutium, or whatever the name was, in a trice; in fact, if Sir
Jamsetsee Jeejeeboy came to him for a copy of verses, and

And Gaspar,[23] when the world he left behind,
Had died with less bad Latin on his mind.

215 MEANWHILE—'tis most improbable and true—
I know a man who read Sordello through.
Since then, whatever can this wight befall,
Or bad or good he thinks it comical,

---

hesitatingly alluded to the difficulty of his name, I believe
the poet would answer, in the words of Hoby to his splay-
footed customer, "Sir, be under no anxiety, we could fit a
pickaxe."

> For instance :—vociferance ⎫
>   difference   ⎬
>   stiffer hence ⎭
>   vestiment ⎫
>   Testament ⎭

Mr. Browning himself very frankly describes the nature of
his inspiration in the poem of " Christmas Eve."

> " A tune was born in my head last week,
> Out of the thump thump and shriek shriek
> Of the train, as I came up from Manchester,
> While it only made my neighbour's haunches stir;
> Finding in him no musical sprout
> As in me to be jolted out."

23 Gaspar Orelli, the learned editor of Horace.

c 2

Even a wedding, or a funeral.

220   His wife recovered from a three days' trance
        Like Dorcas; both his bankers broke at once;
        His mistress jilted him; his son forsook
        Law for the Muse; his daughter wrote a book:
        His country, succoured at an awkward pass,
225   Bade Marochetti libel him in brass :[26]
        Sure *this* would harlequins and clowns appal,
        But he, he laughs at *this*, he laughs at all.
        He laughs in Parliament at Ayrton's[27] speeches.
        He laughs in Church when Canon Wordsworth preaches;
230   Has e'en been known to call Burnand[28] grotesque.
        Has half been thought to smile at a burlesque.

---

[26] Lord Elgin used to be abused for despoiling Greece in order to adorn England. I wish the Greeks would retaliate. But the hope is chimerical; barbarian indeed would be the conqueror who could rob London of her statues.

[27] Member for the Tower Hamlets, and supposed by some to be the weightiest man now before the public, except the gentleman who writes the theological articles for the Pall Mall Gazette.

[28] One of the rabble of punsters that at present infest our stage. Are there no crossings for these gentlemen to sweep,

He laughs at Life, while here he draws his breath,
And only bides his time to laugh at Death.

But graver themes demand a sterner lay,
235 And every thought of laughter dies away ;
High o'er a desk a haunting shade appears,
And frowns the tyrant of my infant years ;
Again I own the magic of the gown,
And hear the awful words, " Sir, take them down.'
240 For lo spruce Matthew[29] dawns upon the view,
And back in terror shrinks a scourged Review ;

---

no party newspapers in which they can write, no private circles
that will be pleased with their dull buffoonery ? It is in vain
for them to attempt to lay the blame on the public taste ; i
have never seen anybody but a theatrical critic laugh at their
contortions ; the public endure them from necessity, not from
choice, and try to forget their contempt for the author in the
liveliness of the spectacle.

[29] Mr. Matthew Arnold, late Professor of Poetry at Oxford, and author of several critical essays, besides two volumes
of poems.

A poaching lad, who kept a private twig,
But deemed himself for punishment too big.
One hand is raised to ward the coming blow,
245   The other wanders to the smart below ;
While features settled to a wavering grin,
Still hide the fright that still he feels within.
And eyes lower doubtful with a sullen light—
Loth to submit, and very loth to fight.
250   Doglike he bays, for baying cheers the heart,
And then—remembers Valour's better part ;
Curlike he whines, and trusts his teeth no more,
But licks the hand he thought to wound before :
While all the school the comedy enjoys,
255   For still he bullies all the weaker boys.

SINCE this smart Arnold reigns without dispute,
And each pretender to the birch is mute,
Let meaner traders to a share agree,
He grandly claims a full monopoly.
260   Should other quacks ancestral records find,
And show prescriptive right to dose mankind,

And yearn to rectify all human ills
With Comtist draughts, and economic pills,
He shuns the contest, dusty at the best,
265 And answers all their prosing with a jest.

A thing that proves he's oligarchical,
For wit's a weapon not possessed by all :
But soon when England's falcon sails are furled,
And Beesley or mad Congreve rule the world,
270 When dukes make shoes, and cobblers boast the gout,

And human nature's turned right inside out,
When each man in his cabbage garden sits,[30]
And one small prison open but for wits ;
Then will the cup of muddy bliss be full,
275 And all be brothers, well informed, and dull ;

And laughing at philosophers will be
Proscribed as outrage on Equality.

TILL then, great Pedagogue, sublimely rule,
Thy wit thy rod, and all the world thy school.

---

[30] See the millennium as described by Dr. Bodichon, who seem
to be a shining light among these soap-and-water philosophers.

250 On " Grand Style," " Culture," still thou lectur'st well,
     And still the flesh is tempted to rebel ;
     Tires of the tedious words in peevish mood,
     As of the Greek too often called the Good :[31]
     Till me at last that preacher's trick of thine
255 Almost persuades to be a " Philistine ;"[32]
     The giants have some faults we can't excuse,
     But are not half so priggish as the Jews.

     Now shift the ground, nor let the game escape,
     But hunt our quarry in another shape.
260 Above not always Phœbus twangs the bow,
     Nor Matthew always plies the rod below ;
     But like a Marquis[33] weary of his state,
     And for a night forgetting to be great,

---

[31] An Athenian peasant is said to have voted for the banish-
ment of Aristides, simply because he was tired of hearing him
called the Just.

[32] Mr. Arnold, I believe, aims at being a citizen of the world.
Was it in the world that he learnt his lecturer's Latin ?

[33] The Marquis Townshend, who so graciously exhibited him-

He grandly doffs the pedagogic vest,
295 And frisks a fool in motley like the rest.
But idle all his pantomimic show,
Constrained and cold the frozen numbers flow ;
He moves on stilts, midst lighter heels forlorn,
Not like the Marquis " to the manner born."
300 Than Balder[34] Woolner boasts no blanker stuff,
And yet God knows that Woolner's blank enough ;
I read them both, and hesitate aghast,
For each seems blankest that I read the last :
While if in rhyme some greater skill he shows,
305 Yet e'en his sonnets much resemble prose.
But should he rules forget and freely sing,
And warmed by genial suns of youth and spring,
The formal trunk put out a sudden spray,
The critic prunes the rebel growth away.

---

self to the vulgar in the part of clown last year, at the Strand
Theatre.

[34] Balder Dead, one of Mr. Arnold's poems.

310 Arnold, farewell—and still a critic be,
  Still steal from Homer all but poetry,
  Mould lifeless copies of the dead antique,
  Write learned stuff that may be verse in Greek ;
  Still chain thy genius in the jail of Time,
315 And born a Briton fly in face of rhyme ;
  In English do what monks in Latin did,[35]
  Be praised by pedants, and by nature chid :
  Yet when thy barbarous metres are forgot,
  When Balder dies, and Mudie knows him not,
320 When Etna hides Empedocles[36] again,
  And e'en thy Merman[37] sleeps beneath the main ;
  Thyrsis[38] shall live ; here Friendship fired the lay,

---

[35] That is to say, transplant classical metres into English, as the monks wrote Latin rhymes.

[36] Empedocles, a Greek sage who leapt down the Crater of Etna, and has been fished up again by Mr. Arnold to be the hero of a poem.

[37] The Forsaken Merman, one of Mr. Arnold's prettiest poems.

[38] Thyrsis, an Elegy on the premature death of the author's friend, Mr. Clough.

The man was there, the critic far away ;

And the sad spirit weeping o'er the grave,

325 Where Fate in envy ravished ere she gave,

Burst its strong bands, a moment wandered free,

And showed the world the bard it lost in thee ;

Thyrsis shall live, and thou in Thyrsis shine,

A critic, pedant, coxcomb, yet divine.

330 BUT hark, the wood with other echoes rings,

And Satyrs gather, for a Satyr sings ;

Their goatish heads are bent in goatish glee.

To doggrel used, and mere debauchery :

For sweet the song, the lyre by Phœbus given,

335 Captive repeats the melodies of heaven.

Their beauteous playmates in these haunts that rove,

Nymphs of the lake, and Dryads of the grove,

Attend too gentle at the name of love.

But fair, proud youths, and maids more fair than they,

340 Creatures whom Titan formed from better clay,[39]

Listen in scorn, and hearing turn away.

---

[39] Compare Juvenal's beautiful lines, Sat. xiv. 31 :—

While men, more callous, laugh or fall asleep,
And I, remembering Atalanta, weep.

WELL—tastes there's no disputing—have your will,
345 Sing on, and filthy once be filthy still.
Yet listen, Swinburne, take a friend's advice,
A friend that's sensible, and not too nice.
Still write of lepers, and pollute your pen,
But still remember that you write for men ;
350 Oh ! be amusing, if you can't be good,
And, unlike Etty,[40] sometimes stir the blood :
'Tis scarcely heaven to sing in Holywell,
But 'tis the devil to be dull as well ;
And lithe long lips whose kisses burn and bite,
355 Fierce arms that smite and slay, or slay and smite.

" Unus et alter,
Forsitan hæc spernant juvenes, quibus arte benignâ,
Et meliore luto finxit præcordia Titan."

[40] I never could help laughing at this painter's pictures : his
huge fat women looked so forlorn in their nakedness, that any
other sentiment but that of mirth was, even in a boyish spectator, impossible.

"The bright light feet, the splendid supple thighs,"
Doves, loves, blood, blushes, serpents, sobs, and sighs.
These fleshy raptures, even you must own,
Are flat to rakes before their beards have grown ;
360 And maudlin ——, weeping o'er the bowl,
Laments and feels his carcase holds a soul.

IF flinty nature hears, and half complies,
And gives cold lust, but passion still denies ;
And love with you, like aldermen's delight,
365 Is just a habit, or an appetite,
Yet make of this what surely may be made,
At least, be plain, and call a spade a spade,
For who'll be satisfied with words alone,
With you in verse, or feebler Scott in stone !
370 Words you have plenty, and the words are fine,
But put some meaning in the liquorish line.
For round you gather a confiding crew.
Of nymphs, and revellers whom the nymphs pursue :
Ingenuous souls who, eager to be taught,
375 Think speech was granted to reveal the thought,

But find their error, when you mount the stairs,

The hungry congregation sweats and stares ;

Yet waits in patience, panting to be fed,

Gets store of scorpions, but little bread ;

380 Hears of " delight's desire, desire's delight,"

Of biting mouths, and " bare throats made to bite,"

Pangs without number, raptures without end,

And more than e'er a —— can comprehend :

Till Julia ponders o'er your Lampsacenes,

385 And Clara asks her lovers what it means.

Still when the sermon ends, they rise to go,

Curious, yet half-contented not to know ;

Like other fanatics, whose faith is strong,

Humble, and satisfied 'tis something wrong."

390 TRUCE to this prate, I would not leave you so,

Spurn me, or hate, yet hear me ere I go ;

Cold blame, and colder courtesies apart,

I speak a brother to a brother's heart.

" A fact.

What wonder cast upon this tedious time,

395 Curst with the curse of genius and of rhyme ;

A minstrel exiled in the tents of Prose,

Where tuneless slaves cant virtue through the nose ;

What wonder youth, life, genius should rebel,

And sick of Eden, call for fruit from Hell,

400 Reject the cup whence happiness is spilt,

And seek a dull forgetfulness in guilt !

Yet. though your lips are red with Circe's wine,

And, scorning fools, you stoop to herd with swine ;

Not this the field for Atalanta's knight,

405 The glorious son of Phœbus and of light :

Far other queen, and other wreaths are due,

Yours are your ballads, but they are not you :

Again I ponder till the lamp burns low,

Althea's crime. and Meleager's woe ;

410 Althea, by her hate, her love undone,

The mourner, mother, slayer of her son ;

And you I single from the nameless dead,

And claim the fadeless laurel for your head.

Hence, loathly shapes! and nightborn dreams away!
415 Freed from the rank mists soars the lord of day;
    So Swinburne soars, again attempts the skies,
    And other Atalantas[12] shall arise;
    Still shall he soar, transcendent o'er the sphere,
    And reign the monarch of our sunless year.

420 NEXT 'neath his dramas, Taylor staggers in,
    And pains and perils for my stairs begin;
    Last of the sons of poor Melpomene,
    And heaviest of a heavy family.
    All ye, that cherish piously a life,
425 Dear to your country, creditor, or wife,
    Or whom mere habit basely tempts to live,

---

[12] Mr. Swinburne is bound to fulfil the splendid promise of his first play, if only to show that my simile has not run away with me. Atalanta has the disadvantage of being the production of an Englishman, who is throughout trying, much to the delight of the critics and antiquarians, to write as if he was a Greek, and altogether smells somewhat too much of the lamp; but, for all that, it is a noble poem. And what must be the force of a genius that is not obscured even by extinct modes of thought and barbarous idioms?

Give ear, and take the warning that I give.

If Taylor skates, the treacherous sport forbear ;

Cross not a bridge, if Taylor lingers there ;

430 Walk if he rides, nor jeopardise a limb ;

And sooner sail with Jonah than with him :

Where fate is sure, 'tis folly not to fear,

And go not e'en on solid earth too near.

Of all his plays " Van Artevelde" 's the best,

435 A few read this, no mortal reads the rest ;

Of all the plays with which my memory's curst,

'Tis true " Van Artevelde " is not the worst.

Great Philip, soberly his course he ran,

A philosophic and self-governed man

440 In love, in hate, in every point but one,

And there the curb was loosened or undone.

He talked---left others worship, pomp and pelf,

But talking kept as sacred to himself—

Lord, how he talked ! of all the wights I know,

445 Few talk so long, and no one talks so slow ;

3

So Richter's[13] horse, the wonder of the way,

Rid by a German thinker, *walked* away :

The thinker pulled, but still he pulled in vain ;

For help he cried, but all his cries disdain ;

450 To stop the creature 'twas beyond his power,

Or make him go one other mile the hour :

So, spent and faint, we let our anger fall,

And think it grace that Philip stops at all.

Once off, no pity can that tongue restrain,

455 And when he breathes, 'tis but to start again.

As at the chase, when Majesty was near,

'Twas treason if a courtier struck the deer ;

If others speak, no quarter will he give,

But deems it insult to prerogative ;

[13] I think it is Richter that tells the story of the horse that *walked* away with a philosopher. This animal had the peculiarity of being utterly indifferent to either curb or spur; nothing could induce it either to go out of its walk, or to stop. It was useless for the rider to cry for help, as people only thought him mad, when they saw the tranquil pace at which the beast was going.

460 Makes war, makes peace, makes love[44] in monologue,
And scents a rebel in a dialogue.

Behold him, victor, safe from war's alarms,
And blest in love's and Adriana's arms !
On pleasure bent he keeps a ruler's mind,[45]
465 Nor leaves one duty unperformed behind :
At mercy's call he stiffens into rock,
And firm sends out Lord Occo to the block ;
Next melting[46] greets his mistress with the line,
Now, Adriana, I am wholly thine.

---

[44] Philip is certainly the prosiest lover in the whole realm of fiction.

[45] Compare Mrs. Gilpin :—

> "For though on pleasure she was bent,
> She had a frugal mind."

[46] See the following lines at the end of the First Part of " Philip Van Artevelde " :—

"ADRIANA :

Oh, spare him ! speak not now of shedding blood,
Now in this hour of happiness ! Oh, spare him !
Vengeance is God's, whose function take not thou ;
Relent, Van Artevelde, and spare his life.

3 *

470 Then when she died some decent tears he shed,
And comfort found with Elena instead.

ALAS! too oft the richest minds and hearts
Are ruined by the greatness of their parts;
Drain nature's wine too rashly to the lees,
475 And destined heroes sink to debauchees,

PHILIP:

Not though an angel plead. Vengeance is God's,
But God doth oftentimes dispense it here
By human ministration. To my hands
He rendered victory this eventful day
For uses higher than my happiness.
Let Flanders judge me from my deeds to-night,
That I from this time forth will thus proceed,
Justice, with mercy tempering where I may,
But executing always. Lead him out. (Occo *is led out.*)
Now, Adriana, I am wholly thine."

It would have been weakness to have pardoned this scoun-
drelly assassin; it is brutal to order his execution and make
love in the same breath. But Philip is a philosopher, and
has his feelings almost as perfectly trained as Fielding's Blifil.
Thwackum would have triumphed in the piety displayed in
this speech, and Square would have been dissolved in emotion
at the name of justice, which, by-the-bye, was his pupil's
great virtue.

Surpassed by those, whose natural gifts were bad,
Who wisely husbanded what gifts they had.
Yet, better far. such ruin'd wreck to be,
Than this cold compound of philosophy.
480 And you, that in your narrow rules confin'd,[17]
Say mastering passion speaks a feeble mind ;

---

[17] Mr. Taylor, in his preface to " Philip Van Artevelde,"
after proving to the best of his ability, that prose is more
poetical than poetry. proceeds to the following remarks on Lord
Byron :—

" Lord Byron's conception of a hero is an evidence not
only of scanty materials of knowledge from which to construct
the ideal of a human being, but also of a want of perception
of what is great or noble in our nature. His heroes are
creatures abandoned to their passions, and essentially, therefore,
weak of mind. Strip them of the veil of mystery, and the
trappings of poetry. resolve them into their plain realities,
and they are such beings as, in the eyes of a reader of mascu-
line judgment. would certainly excite no sentiment of admiration, even if they did not provoke contempt. When the
conduct and feelings attributed to them are reduced to prose
and brought to the test of a rational consideration, they must
be perceived to be beings in whom there is no strength except
that of their intensely selfish passions, in whom all is vanity ;
their exertions being for vanity under the name of love or

Know, if 'tis brightest, happiest to succeed,
Still it is something in such strife to bleed ;

---

revenge, and their sufferings for vanity under the name of
pride. If such beings as these are to be regarded as heroical
where in human nature are we to look for what is low in sentiment and infirm in character?"

To all this I shall only observe that Lord Byron never pro-
fessed " to construct ideals of human beings " (that is Mr. Taylor's business), but expressly stated, again and again, that his
Comrads and Laras were equally guilty and unfortunate. Next,
the demand that poetical conceptions shall be " stripped of their
poetry and reduced to prose," may seem too absurd to be con-
sidered ; yet, even if this be done, Lord Byron's heroes will
not, to any one that knows anything of human nature, appear
" puerile creations." What Mr. Taylor's " reader of mascu-
line judgment," might think of them, I am not curious to in-
quire : perhaps he would be able to look with contempt on
Milton's " Satan," and Homer's " Achilles."

Mr. Taylor backs up his prose with some verses :—

" Then learned I to despise that far-famed school,
    Who place in wickedness their pride, and deem
Power chiefly to be shown where passions rule,
    And not where they are ruled ; in whose new scheme
Of heroism, self-government should seem
A thing left out, or something to contemn,

Nobler to die, or living bear the scar,
485 Than coldly stand a neutral to the war.

Whose notions, incoherent as a dream,
Make strength go with the torrent, and not stem,
For ' wicked and thence weak,' is not a creed for them.

"I left these passionate weaklings, I perceived
What took away all dignity from pride ;
All nobleness from sorrow, what bereaved
E'en genius of respect, they seemed allied
To mendicants, that by the highway side
Expose their self-inflicted wounds, to gain
The alms of sympathy—far best denied—
I heard the sorrowful sensualist complain,
If with compassion, not without disdain."

I don't think this needs any comment ; and my readers must
be as hasty as I am, to bid farewell to this bourgeois criticism,
of a man whose poems are the chief glory of our century, and
whose very faults betrayed the greatness of his soul. Of all
our English poets there are, to my mind, three, and three only,
whose genius is wholly untinctured by pedantry, and who draw
their inspiration directly from life and nature. I mean, of
course, Shakespeare, Burns, and Byron ; and, putting aside Milton, who may be said to stand by himself, it is next to Shakespeare, I predict, that posterity will rank Lord Byron. Mean-

" Weak, selfish," say you, Shakespeare thought not so.
Was Juliet selfish ? weak was Romeo ?

---

while, thanks to the efforts of a school of timid and shallow
critics, he is nowhere so little honoured as in his own country ; but in other lands, to use his own words, his strains :—

> " Have found the fame these shores refuse,
>
>   His place of birth alone is mute."

In brief, he is one of the few of our writers who have an Eu-
ropean reputation. As was said of him by the greatest of his
contemporaries :—

" At present, we can only console ourselves with the convic-
tion that his country will at length recover from that violence
of invective and reproach which has been so long raised against
him, and learn to understand that the dross and lees of the age
and the individual, out of which the best have to elevate themselves, are but perishable and transient, while the wonderful
glory to which he has in the present, and through all future
ages, elevated his country, will be as boundless in its splendour
as it is incalculable in its consequences. Nor can there be any
doubt that the nation which can boast of so many great names,
will class BYRON among the first of those through whom she
has acquired such glory."

Elsewhere he says that "his unfathomable qualities are not
to be reached by words."

I chanced on this quotation just as I was sending these notes

Was Hamlet base? Othello vain? and he,

Who, falling deepest, fell an Antony,

490 And left, the victor of a thousand harms,

A Roman's honour in a harlot's arms—

If these are fit to be contemned, say,

Who would not be contemptible as they !

'T is well, life, passion, nature still abuse,

495 And glory's bays to Byron's[13] shade refuse ;

-----

to the press. Against the number and weight of Lord Byron's detractors, the lance of a tyro like myself could make but little impression. But, with Goethe on my side, I can ask :—

"ἀρκέσει, ἠέ τιν' ἄλλον ἀμύντορα μερμηρίξω ;"

As for the accusations that he was possessed by "an absorbing and contracting self-love," and that "his misanthropy, like his tenderness, was probably assumed for purposes of effect," those who make them can scarcely have read his life. Study his writings, his history, where will you find a more genuine, nay, a more recklessly truthful man ? As to his selfishness, whose distress did he ever turn a deaf ear to? and in what cause did he die ?

[13] As to the assertion that Lord Byron was "in knowledge merely a man of belles lettres, and never applied himself to

Out Wordsworth Wordsworth, this is Phœbus' curse,

And be preposterous where he was perverse ;

That verse is prose was all he had to tell,

You that 'tis prose, and abstract prose[49] as well :

500 Write more, write longer dramas, do your worst,

And froglike vie with Shakespeare till you burst ;

Each reader damns the never-ending stave,

And kingly Byron triumphs in his grave.

--- --- ---

such studies as would have tended to the cultivation of his reasoning powers, and the enlargement of his mind ;" in the first
place to be a man of belles lettres means more than the critic
seems to imagine ; in the second, great poets have generally
studied men more than books. Further, Lord Byron sometimes shows, as in his speech on the "Nottingham Frame
Breaker's Bill," that even on subjects which he did not profess,
he had sounder and more philosophical views than many of his
contemporaries.

[49] Compare Mr. Taylor's dictum that " no man can be a very
great poet, who is not also a great philosopher." I believe the
converse to be nearer the truth : Aristophanes, Hobbes, and
Locke are instances in point.

B<small>UT</small> hush, admire ! a Laureate strikes the strings,

505 And praises Albert for begetting kings ;

Tells us how Enoch left his home and wife,

And came, when least expected, back to life :

How Edith, Maud, and fifty maidens more,

Whom ladies proud to landed scoundrels bore,

510 Died of their love, or else that love forgot,

And straight espoused a sportsman or a sot :

While their bard lived another jilt to woo,

Composed a poem, and forgot them too.

But that it's wrong for girls to disobey,

515 And poets must be moral now a-day,

I wonder why they did not run away.

O<small>R</small> how a clerk, *but gently born and bred,*

Turned round, and broke a medicine-glass[50] in bed,

---

[50] From the " City Clerk" :—

" Nay," said the kindly wife to comfort him,

" You raised your arm, you tumbled down and broke

The glass with little Margaret's medicine in it ;

And, breaking that, you made and broke your dream."

Snored, started, groaned, then dreamed a dream of Life.
520 And told the tedious vision to his wife :
Who also dreamed, and piously inclined,
Revenged herself upon her spouse in kind :
I know not what's the music of the spheres,[51]
But 'twas a discord to my carnal ears.

525 SEE next the huge Geraint, Bœotian lord,
Great at the fight, but greater at the board ;
Whose foes go down whene'er his lance he lowers,
Who eats the dinner of a field of mowers ;[52]
Who when Earl Doorm had eaten all he would,
530 That is, when Doorm had eaten all he could,

---

[51] From the " City Clerk" :—
   " Sphere-music such as that you dreamed about."

[52] In the characters in Mr. Tennyson's " Idylls," as in Monsieur Florian's pastorals, the habits of one class or age are somewhat incongruously joined with the sentiment of another. For instance, Geraint fights and eats like a Homeric champion, but talks and thinks like the hero of a modern novel.

Leaps up, though lying on a shield half dead,
And sends a faulchion flashing through his head.
Thanks to the bard whose sacred song declares
That there were ruffians e'en before Tom Sayers.
535 O could Geraint again his feats rehearse,
And strike in earnest as he strikes in verse,
He'd swell the volume of great Tyrwhitt's cares,
And Mace would tremble for the belt he wears.

 ꞁ IME fails to tell how Percivale got drunk,
540 And waged unequal battle with a punk :
Or how the sweet Sir Sagramore was laid,
A stainless man beside a stainless maid :
Modest as Pickwick with the morn he fled,
The brute world howling forced him back to bed :
545 What though the pair were lying cheek by jowl,
The brute world truly had no cause to howl,
Sure in that court the youth must virtuous be,
Where aged lechers prate of purity.
And so farewell to Vivien's naughty tales,
550 I'm told the custom still obtains in Wales.

BUT cease ! let Folly for a space refrain,
And doff his tall cap as he greets Elaine ;
In fancy's fiery realms he's wandered long,
Marked many a sprite, and paused at many a song ;
555 Wept, wondered, laughed, as crossed in peace or strife
The players in the comedy of Life :
Much has he seen, but nought there was to see,
So spotless, fair, and piteous as she.

PEACE to her shade—now shake the bells once more,
560 Nor keep a hero waiting at the door.
For Arthur comes—not he of ancient fame—
A selfless, stainless shadow of a name :
Robed in red samite, worn by him alone,
Without it, not so *easy to be known* ;
565 A gentleman from Progress' mint is he,
Brand-new, and plated by morality.
Dame Nature stares at this her bastard son,
And sees her lawful progeny outdone,
And proved herself a bungler at the trade,
570 By that perfection which she never made.

She stares and grasps her chisel in her hands,
And flies to ruder and less finished lands ;
Where what she strikes out on her random plan,
May breathe and still pass muster as a man.
575 There (where ! heaven knows,) her busy shop she rears,
And England leaves her tailors and her shears.

BUT sure, if Arthur e'er comes back to men,
As all true Britons wish him back again,
Before he kicks Disraeli down the stairs,
580 Or exiles Gladstone and the doctrinaires,
He'll ask the poet for an explanation,
Or bring his action for a defamation.

NEXT there's a swarm of insects on the wing,
Inspired by idlesse, puberty and Spring ;
585 As reverend Watts avers that puppies do,
They sing because " it is their nature to ;"
Forgetting still, though plain the thing appears,
If they have tongues, that other folk have ears.

48   *HORSE AND FOOT;*

Some plunder Wordsworth thro' each shining hour.
590 Others, as Owen[53] fly from flower to flower,
　　Whatever author graced their schoolboy shelves ;
　　And others copy no one but themselves ;
　　A savage folk, yet honestest of all,
　　And e'en in dulness most original.

595 YET for all this there's reason and excuse,
　　Nor bad the thing, but bad the thing's abuse.
　　Mumps, Chicken-pox, a score of these there be,
　　Affections natural to infancy,
　　The Measles, Whooping-cough, and Poetry—
600 And when they're children that the clamour make,
　　E'en tho' they keep the neighbourhood awake,
　　We take the matter as a thing of course,
　　And think their crying only proves their force.
　　We were boys once, nor 'scaped the common strife,
605 But 'tis the devil when they whoop for life.

---

[53] Mr. Owen Meredith, author of " Clytemnestra," " The
Earl's Return," " Lucile," " The Wanderer," and other poems

This Owen does, by manhood but made bolder,
And whoops the wilder as he grows the older.
An early blight on Owen's being hung,
His heart was old, although his day was young;
610 Champagne he drank, but could not soothe his grief,
He flirted, found in flirting no relief:
At last, as children, tired of cakes and play,
Kill flies to while the tedious hours away,
Grown fierce, he seeks distraction for his mind,
615 And finds it in the torment of his kind.
One moment, maundering in a classic strain,
And Agamemnon[54] murdering again,
The next, he bears on meaner cares intent,
Command in Browning's ragged regiment;
620 Rakes stews and jails for words to serve his turn,
And drills the miscreants in the Earl's Return.[55]

---

[54] In his " Clytemnestra."

[55] The " Earl's Return," an echo of Mr. Browning's spirited poem, " The Flight of the Duchess."

4

Then fired by high ambition for the nonce,

To shine bad novelist and bad bard at once,

Sudden he gives his lumbering jade the heel,

625   And jolters through the sorrows of Lucile.[56]

And last a Wanderer,[57] confident of wing,

Singing the noblest subject man can sing,

Scornful he flings his puppets on the shelf,

And boldly soars the Laureate of himself.

630   N EXT Kingsley's[58] *being bubbles into song,*

Why ! Memory, why the splashing sounds prolong !

Kingsley, the stout Apostle of our time,

Now sinks in blank verse, and now rolls in rhyme,

Potent in both, but most of all prefers

635   To flounder, whalelike, in Hexameters :

--- - - ---   —   —

[56] "Lucile," a sort of novel in singularly rugged verse.

[57] The volume entitled "The Wanderer," consists of a series of short poems; the hero throughout is Mr. Owen Meredith.

[58] Mr. Kingsley has written "Andromeda," a poem in hexameter verse, and other shorter pieces.

While sighing dolphins[59] wanton o'er the tides,

Smit with his maidens and their long white sides.

The horrid metre, indiscreet and hot,

A drunken Pedant upon Discord got,

640 Deep in a cave,[60] where Prosody was not.

All nature groaned, while Dulness gave the sign,

And on their hill-top shrieked aloud the Nine.

[59] From his " Andromeda " :—

> " the wantoning dolphins
> Sighed as they plunged full of love."

and

> " Cold on the cold sea-weeds lay the long white sides of the
> maiden."

[60] Compare Virgil's Æneid :—

> " Speluncam Dido dux et Trojanus eamdem
> Deveniunt. Prima et Tellus et pronuba Juno
> Dat signum : fulsere ignes et conscius æther
> Connubiis ; summoque ulularunt vertice Nymphæ.
> Ille dies primus leti primusque malorum
> Causa fuit. Neque enim specie famave movetur
> Nec jam furtivum Dido meditatur amorem :
> Conjugium vocat ; hoc prætexit nomine culpam."

Sure on that day the fated time began,

Foretold by prophets[61] and long feared by man.

645 When on a throne the goddess shall be seen,

And over willing subjects reign a queen.

Yet on the birth too gracious Arnold[62] smiled,

And kinglike stood godfather to the child :

---

[61] The reign of Dulness prophesied in the Dunciad.

[62] It is fair to mention that Spenser set him the example, as is shown by the following letter to Gabriel Harvey :—

"I like your late English hexameters so exceedingly well, that I also enure my pen something in that kind, which I find, indeed, as I have often heard you defend in word, neither so hard nor so harsh but that it will easily and fairly yield itself to our mother tongue. The only or chiefest hardness which seemeth is in the accent; which sometime gapeth, and, as it were, yawneth, ill-favouredly, coming short of that it should, and sometime exceeding the measure of the number; as in *Carpenter*, the middle syllable being used short in speech, when it shall be read long in verse seemeth like a lame gosling, that draweth one leg after her; and *Heaven*, being used short as one syllable, when it is in verse stretched out with a diastole, is like a dog that holdeth up one leg. But it is to be won with custom, and rough words must be subdued with use."

He subjoins two Elegiacs " which I translated to you in bed the last time we lay together in Westminster :—

While leaden Cayley[63] snuffed the approach of fate,
650 And sate him down in triumph to translate.
But Kingsley, Kingsley, whence can Kingsley be!
Who o'er dead journals pens an elegy,[64]
Writes odes, and writes them to the blighting East,[65]
The wind that's good for neither man nor beast :
655 Nor man, nor beast the sturdy prophet bore,
But some lone crag upon some Arctic shore,
And wolves admiring nursed with milk and gore.

'That which I eat did I joy, and that which I greedily gorged;
As for those many goodly matters left I for others.'"

[63] Mr. C. B. Cayley, author of "Specimens from Lucretius in English Hexameters," and other barbarous actions of the like kind. The only atrocity that I see left for him is to naturalise the Spenserian stanza in Latin, and put the "Fairy Queen" into Latin rhymes.

[64] See the poem entitled "On the Death of a Certain Journal." It seems that it was yawned to death.

[65] Mr. Kingsley really has written an "Ode to the East Wind," and not such a bad one either.

Thus in a rock[66] a pining wife he finds,

And likes the East wind best of all the winds,

660 Since first, like Orson, from his wilds he ran,

And came to shame the puny race of man.

MEEK Oxford called, and Francis[67] swift arose,

Verse his profession, but his practice prose.

Tho' not to him Apollo's harp be given,

665 Nor large his portion of the fire of Heaven,

Yet there is this, and this redeems his lay,

'Tis most unlike its brethren of to-day ;

Where ceaseless fall, whate'er the theme has been,

Words, idle words, I know not what they mean.

670 In short, I've read his book from end to end,

And what I praise not still can comprehend.

---

[66] On a rock that gleams beneath the sunshine, but whose seaweed is drooping, being forsaken by the sea :—

"So many a wife for cruel man's caresses

Must inly pine and pine, yet outward bear

A gallant front to this world's gaudy glare."

[67] Sir Francis Doyle, author of "The Return of the Guards." and other poems ; also Professor of Poetry at Oxford.

In better days men loved their liquor fine,

Nor mud admired in poets or in wine.

Did gifts of puzzling to a wight belong ?

675 He turned his wits to riddling, not to song ;

Or if more thoughtful and more puzzling still,

Northward he hied, and lectured on Freewill.

As Avon clear let Shakespeare's waters run,

Let Byron soar an eagle to the sun ;

680 Our bards,[68] more prudent, mostly walk by night,

And like Imposture ever fly the light,

Nor risk detection 'mongst Aurora's brood,

But skulk beneath the shadow of the wood.

Great may their thought, and vast their meaning be,

685 'Tis vain to question what one cannot see ;

And real perhaps the something that they think,

Though like the cuttlefish it 'scapes in ink.

[68] Our living poets are, it must be admitted, detestably obscure. Indeed, some of them seem to plume themselves on this quality, knowing perhaps, that the mystery of the oracle is sometimes accepted by the vulgar as a proof of its inspiration.

YET to Experience Charity must bow,

And sadly wise I register a vow,

690 Curst be this hand, and blighted be this pen,

If I with Cluvien[69] nutting go again !

Nuts did I get, and cracking did begin,

Broke half my teeth, and maggots found within.

NEXT tuneful Houghton[70] brings a tasteful toil,

695 Let loftier Houghton share the praise of Doyle.

NOW thro' these shadows looms a real man,

Nature his art, and pleasing all his plan.

If there be one, and many there must be,

\   Sick of prose-verse and tradesmen's tragedy,

700 Who keeps a place for Fancy in his heart,

And scorns the new photography of Art :

Or he by dull Analysis made sad,

By Faith fall'n sick, and drivelling Doubt run mad :

---

[69] Cluvienus, a poetaster mentioned by Juvenal. Any modern bard whose conscience reproaches him may take the compliment to himself.

[70] Lord Houghton, author of several short pieces.

Who in each bard a puling sophist fears,

710 And, like the adder, wisely stops his ears.

List once again, for Morris[71] weaves the lay,

Morris, the story-teller of our day.

Nor buskined phrase, nor mouthy rant is there,

With point far-fetched, and artifice worn bare ;

715 Tranquil and still his liquid numbers flow,

And, Thames-like, gather volume as they go.

YET next in England win thy Golden Fleece,[72]

Nor haunt for aye the phantom-land of Greece :

For now the gods and goddesses are dead,

720 Ghosts in the Hades of a scholar's head.

Too daring wizard, take thy harp again,

And sing like Homer of thy countrymen.

----

[71] Mr. William Morris, author of "The Life and Death of Jason," a poem which will make its way. He is a disciple of Chaucer, and uses the metre of the "Canterbury Tales."

[72] The winning of the Golden Fleece was Jason's great exploit.

As Nature roamed in Childhood's fields alone,
She heard a voice as careless as her own ;
725 Sudden she turned, and marked Rossetti[73] there,
So playful, sweet, and innocent of air ;
Silent the goddess gazed, then pitying smiled,
And stayed her hand, and left her still a child.

Last the Pedestrians clamour at Fame's door,
730 Three gentlemen, a lady, and no more ;
If more there be that thus unmounted go,
Their names I know not, may I never know !
A smartish roadster Houghton does not lack,
And Francis[74] owns, and Owen rides a hack ;
735 Sometimes he steals it, and sometimes he begs :
E'en Kingsley[75] keeps a something on three legs.

---

[73] Miss Christina Rossetti, authoress of the "Goblin Market," and other short pieces. I never read anything so arch and original as these poems ; they remind one a good deal of Walter Scott's little friend Margery.

[74] Sir Francis Doyle.

[75] And, under the circumstances, goes better than one would expect.

These wisely feel, however fools may talk,
'Tis safer and 'tis easier to walk.

First gentle Ingelow,[76] like Prose at play,
740 No pushing, Patmore ! for the fair make way :
Noblesse oblige, and if your boast is true,
That no one sings so sillily as you ;
Then none can waive so gracefully a right,
'Tis Greatness' privilege to be polite.

745 A RACE there is, was always, will be still,
Say prophets, and say pedants, what they will
A race there is, that thrives in Britain's air,
In France, Rome, Gaza, Sion, everywhere ;
Who, there, or here, help nations to be great.
750 And form the sure foundation of a state :
Whate'er their creed, dress, country, or their name
The same, and, e'en in Ireland, still the same.

---

[76] Miss Jean Ingelow, authoress of the " Story of Doom," and other poems.

Here, in this island, these their habits are—
They read not much, nor care to travel far,
755 Pay taxes, beat their spouses now and then,
Get drunk at times to show they're Englishmen,
Believe in God, like eating what they list,
Love not a gossip or a journalist,
Work hard, wear well, fear nothing but disgrace.
760 Know a good pointer or a pretty face,
Buy in cheap markets, sell again in dear,
Get sons, go shooting i' the fall o' the year,
Dislike quack-doctors, more dislike dissent,
Distrust a wit, and hate an argument,
765 Wonder at times in winter or wet weather,
When two or three sit silent on together,
Who made a pole-cat or a radical?
Or why teetotallers were made at all?
Keep a sleek horse, and, when they can, keep two
770 In short do all things that they ought to do.

Long may they live, and happy may they be!
Still, two things hate they— DEBT and POETRY;

And one thing love—RESPECTABILITY.

But all moves on, the schoolmaster's abroad,

775 And steam has driven the coaches from the road,

They, with the rest, corrupted and refined,

Demand some dissipation for the mind.

Yet Prudence still holds empire in their breast,

Imagination seems a doubtful guest ;

780 Something they want, like Jourdain in his woes,

Safe, fine, and neither Poetry nor Prose.[77]

To these fair Jean, with Patmore, comfort brings.

For them she labours and to them she sings.

Great Longman hails the woman of the time,

785 And blank verse follows on the heels of rhyme,

---

[77] In "The Bourgeois Gentilhomme," Monsieur Jourdain's Master in Philosophy asks him whether his billet to his mistress shall be in verse :—

"M. JOURDAIN. Non, non ; point de vers.

PHILOSOPH.   Vous ne voulez que de la prose ?

M. JOURDAIN. Non, je ne veux ni prose ni vers.

PHILOSOPH.   Il faut' bien que ce soit l'un ou l'autre.

M. JOURDAIN. Pourquoi ?"

Editions to editions still succeed,

The men they buy them, and the women read.

For all necessities of Luxury,

French-masters, Music, and Prose-Poetry—

790 These still the fair, and not the men, regard,

They talk the French, and listen to the bard.

Music is music, be it poor or fine,

And scan or not scan, still a line's a line,

French French, and creditable—bad or good,

795 Nor it, nor verse need e'er be understood.

She sang of married and of marrying men,

And still she pleased, and still she sang again :

Of sermons,[78] rectors, curates, and their wives,

And all the miseries of single lives ;

---

[78] But in this she is not peculiar, nearly every poet preaches now-a-days; Miss Ingelow in "The Brothers," Mr. Tennyson in "Aylmer's Field ;" while Mr. Patmore carries off the palm with a "*Wedding* Sermon," of some thirty pages, remembering, I suppose, Horace's precept :—

"Omne tulit punctum qui miscuit utile dulci."

The actors will be the next in the field.

800 And still on marriage lavished all her art,[79]
She sang—and reached the British matron's heart.

---

[79] See the poem called "Laurence :"—

> "Then the girl in her first youth,
> Married a curate . . . . . .
> Full soon, for happy years are short, they filled
> The house with children."

Curates always do. See "Story of Doom :"—

> "And when two days were over, Japhet said,
> 'Mother, so please you, get a wife for me.
>
> . . . .
>
> Or else I shall be wifeless all my days.
>
> . . . .
>
> Now, therefore, let a wife be found for me.' "

And in the poem called "The Letter L," a father actually comes from the dead to warn his bachelor son in these words :—

> "I say to thee, though free from care,
> A lonely lot, an aimless life ;
> The crowning comfort is not there—
> Son, take a wife."

The son eventually adopts this advice and marries, although his heart has been lost elsewhere. Some years afterwards, his old love meets him, and being something of a flirt, reminds him of his early passion. He answers not very politely :—

> " 'It may be so, for then,' said he,
> 'I was a fool.' "

Also she told the story of the flood,
And mended Scripture in a daring mood ;

———— ————

And then, turning to his wife, observes :—

    " ' My wife, how beautiful you are !'
     Then closer at her side reclined.
    ' The bold brown woman from afar,
     Comes to me blind.

    " ' And by comparison, I see
     The majesty of matron grace,
    And learn how pure, how fair can be
     My own wife's face.' "

A very prudent and sensible gentleman, who liked the solid comforts of life better than its romance; but if poetry is to descend to celebrate such people, the sooner the art becomes extinct the better. Nothing can be more demoralising than such writing. The last lines are laughable enough.

Here is something from "The Supper at the Mill," which Horace Smith might have envied :—

"Mother. And has your speckled hen brought off her
      brood ?
Frances. Not yet ; but that old duck I told you of,
      She hatched eleven out of twelve to-day.
Child. And granny they're so yellow.

How Noah's sons despised the patriarch,
805 How Noah's daughters tittered at his ark,
How Noah's mother-in-law's dread ghost appeared.
As Noah's wife was kissing Noah's beard."
While giants talk broad church divinity,
And Satan proses, proses horribly ;
810 And last, surpassing all apocrypha."

GEORGE.   And Frances, lass, I brought some cresses in :
Just wash them, toast the bacon, break some
eggs,
And let's to supper shortly."

⁶⁰ See "The Story of Doom ;" Niloiya speaks :—
"Husband, I say,

. . . .

. . My mother's ghost came up last night,
Whilst I thy beard held in my hand did kiss,
Leaning anear thee, wakeful through my love,
And watchful of thee till the moon went down."

⁶¹ Miss Ingelow is really too hard upon the devil. She re-
presents the "hero of Paradise Lost," as a feeble and sickly old
snake, who is bullied by the Giants, and whose conversation is
so tedious that even the most hardened sinners would fly his
company.

5

She boldly slanders poor Methuselah,[82]

Talks of his lizards, says he drove a team,

And calmly makes the good old man blaspheme.

My printer tells me, this is not succeeding,

815 On Sundays, though, 'tis very decent reading.

---

[82] See "The Story of Doom." Methuselah speaks :—
    "Did I love
  The lithe strong lizards that I yoked and set
  To draw my car . . .
  What did the enemy, but on a day
  When I behind my talking team went forth,
  . . . .
  What did the enemy but send his slaves —
  Angels, to cast down stones upon their heads,
  And break them?
  My goodly team, my joy, they all are dead ;
  And I will keep my wrath for ever more
  Against the enemy that slew them,
  The great wise lizards.
  And if He crieth, ' Repent, be reconciled,'
  I answer, ' Nay, my lizards ;' and, again,
  If He will trouble me in this mine age,
  ' Why hast thou slain my lizards ?' "

Now Patmore—but you need no ridicule !
Vanquished I bow to the superior fool ;
Out-capped, out-jingled, from his works I quote,
And Patmore[3] leads out Patmore in a note.

---

[3] I quote from " The Angel in the House :"—
   " I woke at three, for I was bid
      To breakfast with the Dean at nine,
   And thence to church, my curtain slid.
      I found the dawning Sunday fine."

   " We, who are married, let us own,
      The bachelor's chief thought in life
   Is—or the fool's not worth a groan—
      To win some woman for his wife.
   I kept the custom, I confess,
      I never went to ball or fête,
   Or show, but in pursuit express
      Of my predestinated mate."

   " But here their converse had an end,
      For crossing the cathedral lawn,
   There came an ancient college friend,
      Who, introduced to Mrs. Vaughan,
   Lifted his hat, and bowed and smiled,
      And filled her handsome face with joy,
   By patting on the cheek her child,
      With ' Is he yours, this noble boy ?'"

820 I CALL to Woolner, Woolner does not hear,
    Prose caught him up as lone he lingered here :

      " We daily dine with men who stand
        Among the leaders of the land."

Then there is some one, who, among other trials :—
      " Had ghastly doubts his precious life,
        Was pledged for aye to the wrong wife."

Mr. Vaughan one evening left his family circle for the society
of some authors, but did not like his company :—
      " I said I could not stay to sup,
      Because my wife was sitting up,
      And walked home with a sense that I
      Was no match for that company,
      Smelling of smoke, which, always kind,
      Honoria said she did not mind.
      I sipped her tea, saw baby scold,
      And finger at the muslin fold,
      Thro' which he pushed his nose at last,
      And choked and chuckled, feeding fast."
Faugh !

I conclude with a simile, which I believe refers to Love or
Nature, I don't know which :—
      " That's true, cried I, yet as the worm
        That sickens ere it change ;

Bore him aloft to *paradisal* bowers,
Where little spirits make hot love to flowers ;
And children's cheeks flush ever as they rove,
825 *To rosier redness at the name of Love.*
To take the dreamer from his heaven were hard,
So where I found him, there I'll leave the bard,
Serenely shining on a world of Beauty,
Where Love moves ever hand in hand with Duty.

830 LAST low Buchanan[31] *stumps around the house,*
Strong as a stallion, modest as a mouse.

Or as the pup, that nears the term,
    At which pups have the mange."
I suppose "mange" is a poetical term for "distemper."
Yet this book has gone through four editions. Who the deuce
buys them?

[31] Though the specimen in the text may be enough for most
readers, I quote a few others.
    A girl called " Liz " speaks :—
        " So I was glad, when I began to see,
            That Joe the costermonger fancied me."

Nature has not another simile,

Peace, Satire, peace, and let the monster be.

—————————————————

Then there is a London clerk who has fallen in love with his
fellow lodger, " The Little Milliner :"—

"The plain stuff gown, and collar white as snow,
And sweet red petticoat that peeps below.

. . . .

And thought she is undressing now, and, oh !
My cheeks were hot, my heart was in a glow,
Still comforted, although she did not love me,
Because her little room was just above me."

Then, a rustic bard, who, like many other worthy men :—

" Ne'er seemed easy in his Sunday coat,"

says to his wife :—

" The Lord above is very kind to me,
For he has given me this sweet place and you,
Adding the bliss of seeing soon in print
The verse I love so much."

But so devoted is Mr. Buchanan to :—

"The pathos and the power of common life,"

that he copies even its language :—

" Old Matthew took the book, put on his specs,
And tried to read, but, aye, the specs grew dim."

And sometimes its grammar :—

" But Him above had sorer tasks in store."

Rave on, 'tis well, make hideous earth and sea,
835 Cut prose in lengths, and call it poetry ;

Still, he occasionally, as Burns says, " has at the sublime :"—
" The regions where the round red sun,
Is all alone with God among the snow."
" The crucifixion of the good kind Man,
Who loved the weans, and was himself a wean."
Also :—
" Fathom deep the ship doth lie,
Wreathed with ocean-weed, and shell,
The cod slips past with round white eye."

Here we see the love of truth so honourable to the present generation ; the cod-fish is a touch beyond Shakespeare.

Those who wish to be haunted, as I have been the last fortnight, by a most disgusting picture of the birth of a still-born infant, may turn to " London Poems," p. 219—though I don't advise them to do so.

In one of his poems, Mr. Buchanan says :—
" I wish to God I were lying
Yonder 'mong mountains blue,
Smiling in sweet conceptions,
That were dried from my brow like dew."

I suppose he sweats his conceptions. May Providence fulfil the wish ! Meanwhile I really must apologise to Mr. Woolner for the company in which I have placed him ; he, at all events, always writes like a gentleman.

Adapt, translate, there's nought to suffer new.
We've felt the worst stupidity can do.
Invoked, to you, great Midas from the grave,
Pleased with his suppliants all his discords gave ;
840 Despair, like death, a certain calm ensures,
And future brayings can but copy yours.

THE END.

NEW BOOKS

PUBLISHED BY

JOHN CAMDEN HOTTEN,

74 & 75, PICCADILLY, LONDON, W.

. NOTE.—*In order to ensure the correct delivery of the actual Works, or Particular Editions, specified in this List, the name of the Publisher should be distinctly given. Stamps or a Post Office Order may be remitted direct to the Publisher, who will forward per return.*

THE REALITIES OF ABYSSINIA.

"It is almost a truism to say that the better a country is known the more difficult it is to write a book about it. Just now we know very little about Abyssinia and therefore trustworthy facts will be read with eagerness."—*Times*, Oct. 8.

This day, price 7s. 6d., 400 pages, crown 8vo. cloth neat.

Abyssinia and its People; or, Life in the Land of Prester

John. Edited by JOHN CAMDEN HOTTEN, Fellow of the Ethnological Society. With map and eight coloured illustrations.

"This book is specially intended for popular reading at the present time."

"Mr. Hotten has published a work which presents the best view of the country yet made public. It will undoubtedly supply a want greatly felt."—*Morning Post*.

"Very complete and well digested. A cyclopædia of information concerning the country."—*Publisher's Circular*.

"The author is certainly entitled to considerable *kudos* for the manner in which he has collected and arranged very scattered materials."—*The Press*.

"It abounds in interesting and romantic incident, and embodies many graphic pictures of the land we are about to invade. As a handbook for students, travellers, and general readers, it is all that can be desired."—*Court Journal*.

"A book of remarkable construction, and at the present moment, peculiarly useful—very valuable and very interesting."—*Morning Star*.

Immediately.

New Book by the late Artemus Ward.

A genuine unmutilated Reprint of the First Edition of

Captain Grose's Classical Dictionary of the Vulgar Tongue,
1785.

. Only a small number of copies of this very vulgar, but very curious book, have been printed for the Collectors of "Street Words" and Colloquialisms, on fine toned paper, half-bound morocco, gilt top, 6s.

In Crown 8vo., pp. 650, 7s. 6d.

Caricature History of the Georges; or, Annals of the

House of Hanover, from the Squibs, the Broadsides, the Window Pictures, Lampoons, and Pictorial Caricatures of the Time. By THOMAS WRIGHT, F.S.A.

. Uniform with "History of Signboards," and a companion volume to it. A most amusing and instructive work.

John Camden Hotten, 74 & 75, Piccadilly, London.

In 4to., half-morocco, neat, 30s.

"Large-paper Edition" of History of Signboards. With
SEVENTY-TWO extra Illustrations (not given in the small edition), showing Old London in the days when Signboards hung from almost every house.

In Crown 8vo., handsomely printed, 3s. 6d.

Horace and Virgil (The Odes and Eclogues). Translated
into English Verse. By HERBERT NOYES.

THE NEW "SPECIAL" GUIDE.
200 pages, 24 Illustrations, Bird's-eye View Map, Plan, &c. Crown 8vo., price One Shilling.

Hotten's Imperial Paris Guide. Issued under the
superintendence of Mr. CHARLES AUGUSTUS COLE, Commissioner to the Exhibition of 1851.

⁎ This Guide is entirely new, and contains more Facts and Anecdotes than any other published. The materials have been collected by a well-known French Author, and the work has been revised by Mr. Cole.

A SEQUEL TO THE "SHAM SQUIRE."
New and Enlarged Edition, Crown 8vo., boards, 2s. 6d.

Ireland before the Union. With Revelations from the
Unpublished Diary of Lord Clonmell. By W. J. FITZPATRICK, J.P.

This day, price 1s., 160 pages,

A Visit to King Theodore. By a Traveller returned
from Gondar. With a characteristic PORTRAIT.

⁎ A very descriptive and amusing account of the King and his Court by Mr. HENRY A. BURETTE.

A VERY USEFUL BOOK.
Now ready, in Folio, half-morocco, cloth sides, 7s. 6d.

Literary Scraps, Cuttings from Newspapers, Extracts,
Miscellanea, &c. A Folio Scrap-book of 340 columns, formed for the reception of Cuttings, &c. With Guards.

⁎ A most useful volume, and one of the cheapest ever sold. The book is sure to be appreciated, and to become popular.

A MAGNIFICENT WORK.
Immediately, in Crown 4to., sumptuously printed, £7.

Lives of the Saints. With 50 exquisite 4to. Illuminations,
mostly coloured by hand ; the Letterpress within Woodcut Borders of beautiful design.

⁎ The illustrations to this work are far superior to anything of the kind ever published here before.

In Crown 8vo., uniform with the "Slang Dictionary," price 6s. 6d.

Lost Beauties of the English Language. Revived and
Revivable in England and America. An Appeal to Authors, Poets, Clergymen, and Public Speakers.

> "Ancient words
> That come from the poetic quarry
> As sharp as swords."
> HAMILTON'S *Epistle to Allan Ramsay.*

John Camden Hotten, 74 & 75, Piccadilly, London.

NEW AND GENUINE BOOK OF HUMOUR.
Uniform with Artemus Ward. Crown 8vo., toned paper, price 3s. 6d.

Mr. Sprouts his Opinions.
** Readers who found amusement in Artemus Ward's droll books will have no cause to complain of this humorous production. A Costermonger who gets into Parliament and becomes one of the most "practical" Members, rivalling Bernal Osborne in his wit and Roebuck in his satire, OUGHT TO BE an amusing person.

In 3 vols. Crown 8vo., £1. 11s. 6d.

Melchior Gorles. By Henry Aitchenbie.
The New Novel, illustrative of "Mesmeric Influence," or whatever else we may choose to term that strange power which some persons exercise over others, controlling without being seen, ordering in silence, and enslaving or freeing as fancy or will may dictate.

** "The power of detaching the spirit from the body, of borrowing another's physical courage, returning it at will with (or without) interest, has a humorous audacity of conception about it."—*Spectator.*

POPULAR MEMOIR OF FARADAY.
This day, Crown 8vo., toned paper, Portrait, price 6d.

Michael Faraday. Philosopher and Christian. By the
Rev. SAMUEL MARTIN, of Westminster.
** An admirable résumé—designed for popular reading—of this great man's life.

Now ready, One Shilling Edition of

Never Caught: Personal Adventures in Twelve Successful
Trips in Blockade Running.
** A Volume of Adventure of thrilling interest.

FOLK-LORE, LEGENDS, PROVERBS OF ICELAND.
Now ready, Cheap Edition, with Map and Tinted Illustrations, 2s. 6d.

Oxonian in Iceland; with Icelandic Folk-Lore and Sagas.
By the Rev. FRED. METCALFE, M.A.
** A very amusing Book of Travel.

MR. EDMUND OLLIER'S POEMS.
This day, cloth neat, 5s.

Poems from the Greek Mythology, and Miscellaneous
Poems. By EDMUND OLLIER.
"What he has written is enough, and more than enough, to give him a high rank amongst the most successful cultivators of the English Muse."—*Globe.*

THE NEW RIDDLE BOOK.
New Edition of "An awfully Jolly Book for Parties." On toned paper, cloth gilt, 7s. 6d.; cloth gilt, with Illustration in Colours by G. Doré, 8s. 6d.

Puniana; or, Thoughts Wise and Otherwise. Best Book
of Riddles and Puns ever formed. With nearly 100 exquisitely fanciful drawings. Contains nearly 3,000 of the best Riddles and 10,000 most outrageous Puns, and it is believed will prove to be one of the most popular books ever issued.

Why did Du Chaillu get so angry when he was chaffed about the Gorilla? Why? we ask.

Why is a chrysalis like a hot roll? You will doubtless remark, "Because it's the grub that makes the butter fly!" But see "Puniana."

Why is a wide awake hat so called? Because it never had a nap, and never wants one.

John Camden Hotten, 74 & 75, Piccadilly, London.

A REPRODUCTION IN EXACT FACSIMILE, LETTER FOR LETTER, OF
THE EXCESSIVELY RARE ORIGINAL OF SHAKESPEARE'S
FAMOUS PLAY,

Much Adoe about Nothing. As it hath been sundrie times
publikely acted by the Right Honourable the Lord Chamberlaine his seruants.
Written by WILLIAM SHAKESPEARE, 1600.

** Small quarto, on fine toned paper, half bound morocco, Roxburgho style,
4s. 6d. (Original price 10s. 6d.)

Immediately, in Crown 4to., exquisitely printed, £3. 10s.

Saint Ursula, and the Story of the 11,000 Virgins, now
newly told by THOMAS WRIGHT, F.S.A. With Twenty-five Full-page 4to.
Illuminated Miniatures from the Pictures of Cologne.

** The finest book-paintings of the kind ever published. The artist has just
obtained the gold prize at the Paris Exposition.

New Edition, with large Additions, 15th Thousand, Crown 8vo., cloth, 6s. 6d.

Slang Dictionary. With Further Particulars of Beggars'
Marks.

** "BEGGARS' MARKS UPON HOUSE CORNERS.—On our doorways, and on our
house corners and gate posts, curious chalk marks may occasionally be observed,
which, although meaningless to us, are full of suggestion to tramps, beggars, and
pedlars. Mr. Hotten intends giving, in the new edition of his ' Slang Dictionary'—
the fourth—some extra illustrations descriptive of this curious and, it is believed,
ancient method of communicating the charitable or ill-natured intentions of house
occupants; and he would be obliged by the receipt, at 74, Piccadilly, London, of
any facts which might assist his inquiry."—*Notes and Queries.*

UNIFORM WITH ESSAYS WRITTEN IN THE "INTERVALS OF
BUSINESS."

This day, a Choice Book, on toned paper, 6s.

The Collector. Essays on Books, Authors, Newspapers,
Pictures, Inns, Doctors, Holidays, &c. Introduction by Dr. DORAN.

** A charming volume of delightful Essays, with exquisitely-engraved Vignette
of an Old-Book Collector busily engaged at his favourite pursuit of book-hunting.
The work is a companion volume to Disraeli's "Curiosities of Literature," and to
the more recently published "Book-Hunter," by Mr. John Hill Burton.

"A PERFECT MARVEL OF CHEAPNESS."

Five of Scott's Novels, complete, for 3s., well bound.

Waverley Novels. "Toned Paper." Five Choice Novels
COMPLETE FOR 3s., cloth extra, 850 pp. This very handsome Volume
contains unmutilated and Author's Editions of IVANHOE, OLD MORTALITY.
FORTUNES OF NIGEL, GUY MANNERING, BRIDE OF LAMMERMOOR.

Also, *FIRST SERIES*, Fifth Thousand, containing WAVERLEY, THE MONASTERY,
ROB ROY, KENILWORTH, THE PIRATE. All complete in 1 vol., cloth neat, 3s.

A GUIDE TO READING OLD MANUSCRIPTS, RECORDS, &c.

Wright's Court Hand Restored; or, Student's Assistant
in Reading Old Deeds, Charters, Records, &c. Half-morocco, 10s. 6d.

** A New Edition, corrected, of an invaluable Work to all who have occasio
to consult old MSS., Deeds, Charters, &c. It contains a Series of Facsimiles of
old MSS. from the time of the Conqueror, Tables of Contractions and Abbreviations,
Ancient Surnames, &c.

John Camden Hotten, 74 & 75, Piccadilly, London.

RECENT POETRY.

MR. SWINBURNE'S NEW POEM.

This day, fcap. 8vo. toned paper, cloth, 3s. 6d.

A Song of Italy. By Algernon Charles Swinburne.

₊ The *Athenæum* remarks of this poem :—"Seldom has such a chant been heard, so full of glow, strength, and colour."

Mr. Swinburne's "Poems and Ballads."

NOTICE.—The Publisher begs to inform the very many persons who have inquired after this remarkable Work that copies may now be obtained at all Booksellers, price 9s.

Mr. Swinburne's Notes on his Poems and on the Reviews

which have appeared upon them, is now ready, price 1s.

Also New and Revised Editions.

Atalanta in Calydon. By Algernon Charles Swinburne.
6s.

Chastelard: a Tragedy. By A. C. Swinburne. 7s.

Rossetti's Criticism on Swinburne's "Poems." 3s. 6d.

UNIFORM WITH MR. SWINBURNE'S POEMS.

In fcap. 8vo., price 5s.

Walt Whitman's Poems. (Leaves of Grass, Drum-taps, &c.)
Selected and Edited by WILLIAM MICHAEL ROSSETTI.

₊ For twelve years the American poet Whitman has been the object of wide-spread detraction and of concentrated admiration. The admiration continues to gain ground, as evidenced of late by papers in the American *Round Table*, in the *London Review*, in the *Fortnightly Review* by Mr. M. D. Conway, in the *Broadway* by Mr. Robert Buchanan, and in the *Chronicle* by the editor of the selection announced above, as also by the recent publication of Whitman's last poem, from advance sheets, in *Tinsleys' Magazine.*

In preparation, small 4to. elegant.

Carols of Cockayne. By Henry S. Leigh. [Vers de Société
and humorous pieces descriptive of London life.] With numerous exquisite little designs, by ALFRED CONCANNEN.

Now ready, price 3s. 6d.

The Prometheus Bound of Æschylus. Translated in the
Original Metres. By C. B. CAYLEY, B.A.

Now ready, 4to. 10s. 6d., on toned paper, very elegant.

Bianca: Poems and Ballads. By Edward Brennan.

Now ready, cloth, price 5s.

Poems from the Greek Mythology: and Miscellaneous
Poems. By EDMUND OLLIER.

John Camden Hotten, 74 & 75, Piccadilly, London.

In crown 8vo. toned paper.

Poems. By P. F. Roe.

In crown 8vo. handsomely printed.

The Idolatress, and other Poems. By Dr. Wills, Author
of "Dramatic Scenes," "The Disembodied," and of various Poetical contributions to *Blackwood's Magazine.*

HOTTEN'S AUTHORIZED ONLY COMPLETE EDITIONS.
This day, on toned paper, price 6d.; by post, 7d.

Hotten's New Book of Humour. "Artemus Ward Among the Fenians."

This day, 4th edition, on tinted paper, bound in cloth, neat, price 3s. 6d.; by post, 3s. 10d.

Hotten's "Artemus Ward: His Book." The Author's
Enlarged Edition; containing, in addition to the following edition, two extra chapters, entitled "The Draft in Baldinsville, with Mr. Ward's Private Opinion concerning Old Bachelors," and "Mr. W.'s Visit to a Graffick" (Soirée).

*** "We never, not even in the pages of our best humorists, read anything so laughable and so shrewd as we have seen in this book by the mirthful Artemus."— *Public Opinion.*

New edition, this day, price 1s.; by post, 1s. 2d.

Hotten's "Artemus Ward: His Book." A Cheap Edition,
without extra chapters, with portrait of author on paper cover, 1s.

*** NOTICE.—Mr. Hotten's Edition is the only one published in this country with the sanction of the author. Every copy contains A. Ward's signature. The *Saturday Review* of October 21st says of Mr. Hotten's edition: "The author combines the powers of Thackeray with those of Albert Smith. The salt is rubbed in by a native hand—one which has the gift of tickling."

This day, crown 8vo., toned paper, cloth, price 3s. 6d.; by post, 3s. 10d.

Hotten's "Artemus Ward: His Travels Among the
Mormons and on the Rampage." Edited by E. P. HINGSTON, the Agent and Companion of A. Ward whilst "on the Rampage."

*** NOTICE.—Readers of Artemus Ward's droll books are informed that an Illustrated Edition of His Travels is now ready, containing numerous Comic Pictures, representing the different scenes and events in Artemus Ward's Adventures.

This day, cheap edition, in neat wrapper, price 1s.

Hotten's "Artemus Ward: His Travels Among the
Mormons." The New Shilling Edition, with Ticket of Admission to Mormon Lecture.

THE CHOICEST HUMOROUS POETRY OF THE AGE.

Hotten's "Biglow Papers." By James Russell Lowell.
Price 1s.

*** This Edition has been edited, with additional Notes explanatory of the persons and subjects mentioned therein, and is the only complete and correct edition published in this country.

"The celebrated 'Biglow Papers.'"—*Times.*

John Camden Hotten, 74 & 75, Piccadilly, London.

Biglow Papers. Another Edition, with Coloured Plates
by GEORGE CRUIKSHANK, bound in cloth, neat, price 3s. 6d.

Handsomely printed, square 12mo.,

Advice to Parties About to Marry. A Series of
Instructions in Jest and Earnest. By the Hon. HUGH ROWLEY, and illustrated with numerous comic designs from his pencil.

AN EXTRAORDINARY BOOK.

Beautifully printed, thick 8vo., new, half morocco, Roxburghe, 12s. 6d.

Hotten's Edition of "Contes Drolatiques" (Droll Tales
collected from the Abbeys of Loraine). Par BALZAC. With Four Hundred and Twenty-five Marvellous, Extravagant, and Fantastic Woodcuts by GUSTAVE DORÉ.

*** The most singular designs ever attempted by any artist. This book is a fund of amusement. So crammed is it with pictures that even the contents are adorned with thirty-three illustrations. *Direct application must be made to Mr. Hotten for this work.*

THE ORIGINAL EDITION OF JOE MILLER'S JESTS. 1739. Price 9s. 6d.

Joe Miller's Jests: or, the Wit's Vade-Mecum; a Collection
of the most brilliant Jests, politest Repartees, most elegant Bons Mots, and most pleasant short Stories in the English Language. An interesting specimen of remarkable facsimile, 8vo., half morocco, price 9s. 6d. London : printed by T. Read, 1739.

Only a very few copies of this humorous book have been reproduced.

This day, handsomely printed on toned paper, price 3s. 6d.; cheap edition, 1s.

Hotten's "Josh Billings: His Book of Sayings;" with
Introduction by E. P. HINGSTON, companion of Artemus Ward when on his "Travels."

*** For many years past the sayings and comicalities of "Josh Billings" have been quoted in our newspapers. His humour is of a quieter kind, more aphoristically comic, than the fun and drollery of the "delicious Artemus," as Charles Reade styles the Showman. If Artemus Ward may be called the comic story-teller of his time, "Josh" can certainly be dubbed the comic essayist of his day. Although promised some time ago, Mr. Bilings' "Book" has only just appeared, but it contains all his best and most mirth-provoking articles.

This day, in three vols, crown 8vo., cloth, neat.

Orpheus C. Kerr Papers. The Original American Edition,
in Three Series, complete. Three vols., 8vo., cloth; sells at £1. 2s. 6d., now specially offered at 15s.

*** A most mirth-provoking work. It was first introduced into this country by the English officers who were quartered during the late war on the Canadian frontier. They found it one of the drollest pieces of composition they had ever met with, and so brought copies over for the delectation of their friends.

Orpheus C. Kerr [Office Seeker] Papers. First Series,
Edited by E. P. HINGSTON. Price 1s.

THACKERAY AND GEORGE CRUIKSHANK.

In small 8vo., cloth, very neat, price 4s. 6d.

Thackeray's Humour. Illustrated by the Pencil of George
CRUIKSHANK. Twenty-four Humorous Designs executed by this inimitable artist in the year 1849-40, as illustrations to "The Fatal Boots" and "The Diary of Barber Cox," with letterpress descriptions suggested by the late Mr. Thackeray.

THE ENGLISH GUSTAVE DORÉ.
This day, in 4to., handsomely printed, cloth gilt, price 7s. 6d.; with plates
uncoloured, 5s.

The Hatchet-Throwers ; with Thirty-six Illustrations,
coloured after the Inimitably Grotesque Drawings of ERNEST GRISET.

*** Comprises the astonishing adventures of Three Ancient Mariners, the
Brothers Brass of Bristol, Mr. Corker, and Mungo Midge

"A Munchausen sort of book. The drawings by M. Griset are very powerful
and eccentric."—*Saturday Review.*

This day, in Crown 8vo., uniform with "Biglow Papers," price 3s. 6d.

Wit and Humour By the "Autocrat of the Breakfast
Table." A volume of delightfully humorous Poems, very similar to the mirthful verses of Tom Hood. Readers will not be disappointed with this work.

Cheap edition, handsomely printed, price 1s.

Vere Vereker: a Comic Story. by Thomas Hood, with
Punning Illustrations. By WILLIAM BRUNTON.

*** One of the most amusing volumes which have been published for a long
time. For a piece of broad humour, of the highly-sensational kind, it is perhaps
the best piece of literary fun by Tom Hood.

Immediately, at all the Libraries.

Cent. per Cent. : a Story written upon a Bill Stamp. By
BLANCHARD JERROLD. With numerous coloured illustrations in the
style of the late Mr. Leech's charming designs.

*** A Story of "The Vampires of London," as they were pithily termed in a
recent notorious case, and one of undoubted interest.

AN ENTIRELY NEW BOOK OF DELIGHTFUL FAIRY TALES.

Now ready, square 12mo., handsomely printed on toned paper, in cloth, green
and gold, price 4s. 6d. plain, 5s. 6d. coloured (by post 6d. extra).

Family Fairy Tales: or, Glimpses of Elfland at Heatherston
Hall. Edited by CHOLMONDELEY PENNELL, Author of "Puck on
Pegasus," &c., adorned with beautiful pictures of "My Lord Lion," "King
Uggermugger," and other great folks.

*** This charming volume of Original Tales has been universally praised by the
critical press.

Pansie: a Child Story, the Last Literary Effort of
Nathaniel Hawthorne. 12mo., price 6d.

Rip Van Winkle: and the "Story of Sleepy Hollow."
By WASHINGTON IRVING. Foolscap 8vo., very neatly printed on toned
paper, illustrated cover, 6d.

Anecdotes of the Green Room and Stage; or. Leaves from
an Actor's Note-Book, at Home and Abroad. By GEORGE VANDENHOFF.
Post 8vo., pp 336, price 2s.

*** Includes original anecdotes of the Keans (father and son), the two Kembles,
Macready, Cooke, Liston, Farren, Elliston, Braham and his Sons, Phelps, Buck-
stone, Webster, Charles Matthews, Siddons, Vestris, Helen Faucit, Mrs. Nisbet,
Miss Cushman, Miss O'Neil, Mrs. Glover, Mrs Charles Kean, Rachel, Ristori, and
many other dramatic celebrities.

John Camden Hotten, 74 & 75, Piccadilly, London.

Berjeau's (P. C.) Book of Dogs : the Varieties of Dogs as
they are found in Old Sculptures, Pictures, Engravings, and Books. 1865.
Half-morocco, the sides richly lettered with gold, 7s. 6d.

*** In this very interesting volume are 52 plates, facsimiled from rare old En-
gravings, Paintings, Sculptures, &c , in which may be traced over 100 varieties of
dogs known to the ancients.

This day, elegantly printed, pp. 96, wrapper 1s., cloth 2s., post free.

Carlyle on the Choice of Books. The Inaugural Address
of THOMAS CARLYLE, with Memoir, Anecdotes, Two Portraits, and View
of his House in Chelsea. The "Address" is reprinted from *The Times*,"
carefully compared with twelve other reports, and is believed to be the most
accurate yet printed.

*** The leader in the *Daily Telegraph*, April 25th, largely quotes from the above
" Memoir "

In Fcap. 8vo., cloth, price 3s. 6d. beautifully printed.

Gcg and Magog; or, the History of the Guildhall Giants.
With some Account of the Giants which guard English and Continental Cities.
By F. W. FAIRHOLT, F.S.A. With Illustrations on Wood by the author,
coloured and plain.

*** The critiques which have appeared upon this amusing little work have been
uniformly favourable. The *Art Journal* says, in a long article, that it thoroughly
explains who these old giants were, the position they occupied in popular mytho-
logy, the origin of their names, and a score of other matters, all of much interest
in throwing a light upon fabulous portions of our history.

Now ready, handsomely printed, price 1s. 6d.

Hints on Hats; adapted to the Heads of the People.
By HENRY MELTON, of Regent Street. With curious woodcuts of the
various style of Hats worn at different periods.

*** Anecdotes of eminent and fashionable personages are given, and a fund of
interesting information relative to the History of Costume and change of tastes
may be found scattered through its pages.

This day, handsomely bound, pp. 550, price 7s. 6d.

History of Playing Cards: with Anecdotes of their Use in
Ancient and Modern Games, Conjuring, Fortune-Telling, and Card-sharping.
With Sixty curious illustrations on toned paper. Skill and Sleight-of-Hand ;
Gambling and Calculation ; Cartomancy and Cheating : Old Games and
Gaming-Houses ; Card Revels and Blind Hookey ; Piquet and Vingt-et-un ;
Whist and Cribbage ; Old-fashioned Tricks.

" A highly-interesting volume."—*Morning Post*.

This day, in 2 vols., 8vo., very handsomely printed, price 16s.

THE HOUSEHOLD STORIES OF ENGLAND.

Popular Romances of the West of England ; or. the Drolls
of Old Cornwall. Collected and edited by ROBERT HUNT, F.R.S.

For an analysis of this important work see printed description, which may be
obtained gratis at the publisher's.

Many of the stories are remarkable for their wild poetic beauty ; others surprise
us by their quaintness ; whilst others, again, show forth a tragic force which can
only be associated with those rude ages which existed long before the period of
authentic history.

Mr. George Cruikshank has supplied two wonderful pictures as illustrations to
the work. One is a portrait of Giant Bolster, a personage twelve miles high.

John Camden Hotten, 74 & 75, Piccadilly, London.

Pp. 336, handsomely printed, cloth extra, price 3s. 6d.

Holidays with Hobgoblins; or, Talk of Strange Things.

By DUDLEY COSTELLO. With humorous engravings by GEORGE CRUIKSHANK. Amongst the chapters may be euumerated : Shaving a Ghost ; Superstitions and Traditions ; Monsters ; the Ghost of Pit Pond ; the Watcher of the Dead ; the Haunted House near Hampstead ; Dragons, Griffins, and Salamanders ; Alchemy and Gunpowder : Mother Shipton ; Bird History ; Witchcraft and Old Boguey ; Crabs ; Lobsters ; the Apparition of Mousieur Bodry.

SUPPLEMENTARY VOLUME TO HONE'S WORKS.

In preparation, thick 8vo., uniform with " Year-Book," pp. 800.

Hone's Scrap Book. A Supplementary Volume to the

" Every-Day Book," the " Year-Book," and the " Table-Book." From the MSS. of the late WILLIAM HONE, with upwards of One Hundred and Fifty engravings of curious or eccentric objects.

BARNUM'S NEW BOOK.

Humbugs of the World. By P. T. Barnum. Pp. 320.

crown 8vo., cloth extra, 4s. 6d.

" A most vivacious book, and a very readable one."— *Globe.*

"The history of Old Adams and his grisly bears is inimitable."—*Athenæum.*

"A History of Humbugs by the Prince of Humbugs ! What book can be more promising ? "—*Saturday Review.*

A KEEPSAKE FOR SMOKERS.

This day, 45mo., beautifully printed from silver-faced type, cloth, very neat, gilt edges, price 2s. 6d.

Smoker's Text Pook. By J. Hamer, F.R.S.L. This

exquisite little volume comprises the most important passages from the works of eminent men written in favour of the much-abused weed. Its compilation was suggested by a remark made by Sir Bulwer Lytton :—

" A pipe is a great comforter, a pleasant soother. The man who smokes thinks like a sage and acts like a Samaritan."

** A few copies have been choicely bound in calf antique and morocco, price 10s. 6d. each.

A NEW BOOK BY THE LATE MR. THACKERAY.

The Student's Quarter; or, Paris Life Five-and-Twenty

Years Since. By the late WILLIAM MAKEPEACE THACKERAY. With numerous coloured illustrations after designs made at the time.

** For these interesting sketches of French literature and art, made immediately after the Revolution of 1830, the reading world is indebted to a gentlemen in Paris, who has carefully preserved the original papers up to the present time.

Thackeray: the Humorist and the Man of Letters. The

Story of his Life and Literary Labours. With some particulars of his Early Career never before made public. By THEODORE TAYLOR, Esq., Membre de la Société des gens de Lettres. Price 7s. 6d.

** Illustrated with Photographic Portrait (one of the most characteristic known to have been taken) by Ernest Edwards, B.A.; view of Mr. Thackeray's House, built after a favourite design of the great novelist's ; facsimile of his Handwriting, long noted in London literary circles for its exquisite neatness; and a curious life sketch of his Coat of Arms, a pen and pencil humorously introduced as the crest, the motto, " Nobilitas est sola virtus " (Virtue is the sole nobility).

John Camden Hotten, 74 & 75, Piccadilly, London.

This day, neatly printed, price 1s. 6d. ; by post 1s. 8d.

Mental Exertion: its Influence on Health. By Dr.
BRIGHAM. Edited, with additional Notes, by Dr. ARTHUR LEARED,
Physician to the Great Northern Hospital. This is a highly important little
book, showing how far we may educate the mind without injuring the body.

. The recent untimely deaths of Admiral Fitzroy and Mr. Prescott, whose
minds gave way under excessive mental exertion, fully illustrate the importance
of the subject.

EVERY HOUSEKEEPER SHOULD POSSESS A COPY.

Now ready, in cloth, price 2s. 6d. ; by post 2s. 8d.

The Housekeeper's Assistant; a Collection of the most
valuable Recipes, carefully written down for future use, by Mrs. B——
during her forty years' active service.

As much as two guineas has been paid for a copy of this invaluable little work.

How to See Scotland; or, a Fortnight in the Highlands
for £6.
A plain and practical guide.—Price 1s.

Now ready, 8vo., price 1s.

List of British Plants. Compiled and Arranged by Alex
More, F.L.S.
. This comparative *List of British Plants* was drawn up for the use of the
country botanist, to show the differences in opinion which exist between different
authors as to the number of species which ought to be reckoned within the compass
of the *flora* of Great Britain.

Now ready, price 2s. 6d. ; by post 2s. 10d.

Dictionary of the Oldest Words in the English Language,
from the Semi-Saxon Period of A.D. 1250 to 1300; consisting of an Alphabetical
Inventory of Every Word found in the Printed English Literature of the 13th
Century, by the late HERBERT COLERIDGE, Secretary to the Philological
Society. 8vo., neat half morocco.

. An invaluable work to historical students and those interested in linguistic
pursuits.

The School and College Slang of England; or, Glossaries
of the Words and Phrases peculiar to the six great Educational Establishments
of the country.—Preparing.

This day, in Crown 8vo., handsomely printed, price 7s. 6d.

Glossary of all the Words, Phrases, and Customs peculiar
to Winchester College.
See "School Life at Winchester College," recently published.

Robson; a Sketch, by Augustus Sala. An Interesting
Biography, with Sketches of his famous characters, "Jem Baggs," "Boots at
the Swan," "The Yellow Dwarf," "Daddy Hardacre," &c. Price 6d.

In preparation, Crown 8vo., handsomely printed.

The Curiosities of Flagellation: an Anecdotal History
of the Birch in Ancient and Modern Times : its Use as a Religious Stimulant,
and as a Corrector of Morals in all Ages. With some quaint illustrations. By
J. G. BERTRAND, Author of " The Harvest of the Sea," &c.

John Camden Hotten, 74 & 75, Piccadilly, London.

In 1 vol., with 300 Drawings from Nature, 2s. 6d. plain, 4s. 6d. coloured by hand.

The Young Botanist: a Popular Guide to Elementary
Botany. By T. S. RALPH, of the Linnæan Society.

. An excellent book for the young beginner. The objects selected as illustrations are either easy of access as specimens of wild plants, or are common in gardens.

Common Prayer. Illustrated by Holbein and Albert Durer.
With Wood Engravings of the " Life of Christ," rich woodcut border on every page of Fruit and Flowers; also the Dance of Death, a singularly curious series after Holbein, with Scriptural Quotations and Proverbs in the Margin. Square 8vo., cloth neat, exquisitely printed on tinted paper, price 8s. 6d.; in dark morocco, very plain and neat, with block in the Elizabethan style impressed on the sides, gilt edges, 16s. 6d.

Apply direct for this exquisite volume.

AN APPROPRIATE BOOK TO ILLUMINATE.
. The attention of those who practise the beautiful art of Illuminating is requested to the following sumptuous volume:—

The Presentation Book of Common Prayer. Illustrated
with Elegant Ornamental Borders in red and black, from " Books of Hours " and Illuminated Missals, by GEOFFREY TORY. One of the most tasteful and beautiful books ever printed. May now be seen at all booksellers.

Although the price is only a few shillings (7s. 6d. in plain cloth; 8s. 6d. antique do.; 14s. 6d. morocco extra), this edition is so prized by artists that, at the South Kensington and other important Art Schools, copies are kept for the use of students.

Now ready, in 8vo., on tinted paper, nearly 350 pages, very neat, price 5s.

Family History of the English Counties: Descriptive
Account of Twenty Thousand most Curious and Rare Books, Old Tracts, Ancient Manuscripts, Engravings, and Privately-printed Family Papers, relating to the History of almost every Landed Estate and Old English Family in the Country; interspersed with nearly Two Thousand Original Anecdotes, Topographical and Antiquarian Notes. By JOHN CAMDEN HOTTEN.

By far the largest collection of English and Welsh Topography and Family History ever formed. Each article has a small price affixed for the convenience of those who may desire to possess any book or tract that interests them.

AN INTERESTING VOLUME TO ANTIQUARIES.
Now ready, 4to., half morocco, handsomely printed, price 7s. 6d.

Army Lists of the Roundheads and Cavaliers in the Civil
War.

. These most curious Lists show on which side the gentlemen of England were to be found during the great conflict between the King and the Parliament. Only a very few copies have been most carefully reprinted on paper that will gladden the heart of the lover of choice books.

Folio, exquisitely printed on toned paper, with numerous Etchings, &c., price 29s.

Millais Family, the Lineage and Pedigree of, recording
its History from 1331 to 1865, by J. B. PAYNE, with Illustrations from Designs by the Author.

. Of this beautiful volume only sixty copies have been privately printed for presents to the several members of the family. The work is magnificently bound in blue and gold. These are believed to be the only etchings of an heraldic character ever designed and engraved by the distinguished artist of the name.

Apply direct for this work.

John Camden Hotten, 74 & 75, Piccadilly, London.

Now ready, 12mo., very choicely printed, price 6s. 6d.

London Directory for 1 77, the Earliest Known List of
the London Merchants. See Review in the *Times*, Jan. 22.

*** This curious little volume has been reprinted verbatim from one of the only two copies known to be in existence. It contains an Introduction pointing out some of the principal persons mentioned in the list. For historical and genealogical purposes the little book is of the greatest value. Herein will be found the originators of many of the great firms and co-partnerships which have prospered through two pregnant centuries, and which exist some of them in nearly the same names at this d y. Its most distinctive feature is the early severance which it marks of "goldsmiths that keep running cashes," precursors of the modern bankers, from the mass of the merchants of London.

Now ready, price 5s.; by post, on roller, 5s. 4d.

Magna Charta. An Exact Facsimile of the Original
Document preserved in the British Museum, very carefully drawn, and printed on fine plate paper, nearly 3 feet long by 2 feet wide, with the Arms and Seals of the Barons elaborately emblazoned in gold and colours. A.D. 1215.

*** Copied by express permission, and the only correct drawing of the Great Charter ever taken. Handsomely framed and glazed, in carved oak of an antique pattern, 22s. 6d. It is uniform with the "Roll of Battle Abbey."
A full translation, with Notes, has just been prepared, price 6d.

NEW BOOK BY PROFESSOR RENAN'S ASSOCIATE.

Exquisitely printed, 12mo., cloth, very neat, price 3s. 6d.

Apollonius of Tyana: the Pagan or False Christ of the
Third Century. An Essay. By ALBERT REVILLE, Pastor of the Walloon Church at Rotterdam. Authorized translation.

*** A most curious account of an attempt to revive Paganism in the third century by means of a false Christ. Strange to say, the principal events in the life of Apollonius are almost identical with the Gospel narrative. Apollonius was born in a mysterious way about the same time as Christ. After a period of preparation came a Passion, then a Resurrection, and an Ascension. In many other respects the parallel is equally extraordinary.

In the press, 4to. Part I.

The Celtic Tumuli of Dorsetshire: an Account of Personal
and other Researches on the Sepulchral Mounds of the Durotiges; forming the First Part of a Description of the Primeval Antiquities of the County.

In small 4to. handsomely printed, 1s. 6d.

Esholt in Airedale, Yorkshire: the Cistercian Priory of
St. Leonard, Account of, with View of Esholt Hall.

ANECDOTES OF THE "LONG PARLIAMENT" OF 1645.

Now ready, in 4to., half morocco, choicely printed, price 7s. 6d.

The Mysteries of the Good Old Cause: Sarcastic Notices
of those Members of the Long Parliament that held places, both Civil and Military, contrary to the Self-denying Ordinance of April 3, 1645; with the sums of money and lands they divided among themselves.

*** Gives many curious particulars about the famous Assembly not mentioned by historians or biographers. The history of almost every county in England receives some illustration from it. Genealogists and antiquaries will find in it much interesting matter.

John Camden Hotten, 74 & 75, Piccadilly, London.

Now ready, in 4to., very handsomely printed, with curious woodcut initial letters,
extra cloth, 18s.; or crimson morocco extra, the sides and back covered
in rich fleur-de-lys, gold tooling, 55s.

Roll of Carlaverlock, with the Arms of the Earls, Barons,

and Knights who were present at the Siege of this Castle in Scotland, 26
Edward I., A.D. 1300; including the Original Anglo-Norman Poem, and an
English Translation of the MS. in the British Museum; the whole newly edited
by THOMAS WRIGHT, Esq., M.A., F.S.A.

*** A very handsome volume, and a delightful one to lovers of Heraldry, as it is
the earliest blazon or arms known to exist.

UNIFORM WITH "MAGNA CHARTA."

Roll of Battle Abbey; or, a List of the Principal Warriors

who came over from Normandy with William the Conqueror and settled in this
country, A.D. 1066-7, from Authentic Documents, very carefully drawn, and
printed on fine plate paper, nearly three feet long by two feet wide, with the
Arms of the principal Barons elaborately emblazoned in gold and colours, price
6s ; by post, on roller, 5s. 4d.

*** A most curious document, and of the greatest interest, as the descendants
of nearly all these Norman Conquerors are at this moment living amongst us. No
names are believed to be in this "Battel Roll," which are not fully entitled to the
distinction.
Handsomely framed and glazed, in carved oak of an antique pattern, price 22s. 6d.

Warrant to Execute Charles I. An Exact Facsimile of this

Important Document in the House of Lords, with the Fifty-nine Signatures
of the Regicides, and Corresponding Seals, admirably executed on paper made
to imitate the Original Document, 22 in. by 14 in. Price 2s.; by post, 2s. 4d.
Handsomely framed and glazed, in carved oak of an antique pattern, 14s. 6d.

Now ready.

Warrant to Execute Mary Queen of Scots. The Exact

Facsimile of this Important Document, including the Signature Queen Eliza-
beth and Facsimile of the Great Seal, on tinted paper, made to imitate the
original MS. Safe on roller, 2s.; by post, 2s. 4d.
Handsomely framed and glazed, in carved oak of an antique pattern, 14s. 6d.

In 1 vol., 4to., on tinted paper, with 19 large and most curious Plates in facsimile,
coloured by hand, including an ancient View of the City of Waterford.

Illuminated Charter-Roll of Waterford, Temp. Richard II.

Price to Subscribers, 20s. ; Non-subscribers, 30s.

*** Of the very limited impression proposed, more than 150 copies have already
been subscribed for. Amongst the Corporation Muniments of the City of Waterford is preserved an ancient Illuminated Roll, of great interest and beauty, com-
prising all the early Charters and Grants to the City of Waterford, from the time
of Henry II. to Richard II. Full-length Portraits of each King adorn the margin,
varying from eight to nine inches in length—some in armour and some in robes of
state. In addition are Portraits of an Archbishop in full canonicals, of a Chancellor,
and of many of the chief Burgesses of the City of Waterford, as well as singularly-
curious Portraits of the Mayors of Dublin, Waterford, Limerick, and Cork, figured
for the most part in the quaint bipartite costume of the Second Richard's reign,
peculiarities of that of Edward III. Altogether this ancient work of art is unique
of its kind in Ireland, and deserves to be rescued from oblivion.

John Camden Hotten, 74 & 75, Piccadilly, London.